Kodia

I give thanks to my Ancestors first and foremost for giving me what to write in my dreams. To all the spirits who are in my courts, with you I am everything and with you I am nothing. When I would ask for help to keep writing, YOU kept showing me in my dreams what would happen next.

I dedicate this book to my husband Tom Counts III for all his patience during the times I was writing this. Waking up in the middle of the night when the visions would come to me to write and disturbing his sleep, I want to say thank you! Thank you for all the mountain trips!

To my daughter Laresa Raines and my son Larry Bostic Jr. for telling me that I could do it and that I'm never to old to accomplish my goals. I do this for my two grandchildren Raiquan and Aryeh.

To my beautiful mother, Joanne Seawell, who I received my talent from. You write beautifully as well. To my brother and sisters Phillip, Othaey, Danny and Avia. Look at your big sister work!

To my best friends Tammy-Jones Smith, Cherie Riddick-Jones and Marcell Reid. You ladies have always encouraged me to keep writing and have always had my back no matter what.

To my godchildren Anthony and Carla for always being here for me.

To everyone else my family and friends, thank you for the encouraging words and waiting patiently to read all my works.

Special thanks go to Janae for giving me my first set of elekes and introducing me to Orishas, I would not have broadened my horizon to learn more and become more. You brought me my first message from the spirit world encouraging me to open and allow them to take over my life completely. I still got the original letter, their message! Special thanks go to Papa Joe for introducing me to the Loa's and showing me their houses. Throughout the years you have guided me and helped me to become closer to them.

The Zar cult believes that people at some point in their lives are possessed by at least two jinn, *"masters of the spirit"*. The Kodia has experienced Zar possession and has a working relationship with her spirits. This position is hereditary, passed from mother to daughter or through female members of the family.

Drawing Down the Spirits-The Traditions and Techniques of Spirit Possession

Chapter 1

Kodia

I am running as fast I can through the woods. I do not see what is chasing me, but I know something is behind me. I see a white house up ahead and I know that if I make it to that house, I will be safe. I keep running and then I hear dogs barking at me forcing me to trip over a red brick that was laying in my way. I hurry up and gather myself together to keep moving because if it catches me, I know that I will be trapped and lost forever. I finally make it to the white house and once again as so many times before, I knew that once my feet stepped up on the porch that the ancestors would save me, and my soul would not be lost. The moment I placed my left foot on the porch I was knocked back. I fell hitting the ground with a strong force and I was so scared. What in the hell was that stopping me from my safety point? I tried to get back up and step up on the porch but instantly I was knocked back to the ground. It was as if I no longer had any protection from the ancestors anymore. I could *hear the dog's barks getting louder which meant that it was getting closer to me. I turned my head and looked back at the woods where I had just run from, and I could see a tall dark shadow watching me. It was coming for me. I could see, no feel the dogs beginning to move closer and I began to scream for someone to save me. Suddenly, skeletal hands came out from under the ground and they snatched me under...*I woke up screaming and when I looked down at my gown I was covered in dirt.

This dream was different this time. I keep having the same reoccurring dreams every night but this time the faces of the Ancestors did not show up in the house and they did not save me from what was chasing me. I was so tired of running and even in my dreams I wanted to give up. But the old white house was my safety spot and I knew that the dark shadow that was chasing me could not touch me once I made it there. But this time they did not save me. *They* allowed me to get caught. What the fuck was going on with me?

Ever since I was a small child I was always being chased in

my dreams. Everyone told me that I was born with a veil over my face but even I did not believe that. I knew that as I got older things would come so strong to me and I was always seeing spirits. Especially one dressed in a red cloak. I was used to seeing them but now I was bringing them into my dreams, and what was in my dreams was following me outside of my dreams as well.

I got up out of the bed and walked into the kitchen. I went over to the cabinet opened it and took me a glass down. I walked over to sink and turned on the faucet. As the water began to flow out, I placed three fingers in the glass, and I allowed the water to touch my fingers. My sister told me to always do that to place my energy into the water for my protection. I took the glass to the table and sat it down. I stared into the glass.

As I began staring at the water, I could see bubbles forming inside the glass. At first, they were tiny but then they began to fill the glass. What the fuck? I picked the glass up and it broke in my hands. I jumped up from the table and began moving backwards towards the wall. The table followed me and pinned me against the wall. The faucet at the sink turned on and the water began pulsating out in short bursts. The cabinet doors flung open and my dishes began vibrating. I closed my eyes and let out a loud scream. Suddenly it all stopped!

I opened my eyes, looked around the kitchen and I could not see any spirits. I pushed the table away from me as I grabbed my cell phone sitting on the kitchen counter, and ran out of the house. I tried to call my sister, but she did not answer her phone. I ran to my car, opened the door and crawled into the back seat. I laid back on the seat and closed my eyes silently praying as I fell asleep.

I was awakened by the alarm on my cell phone going off. Friday had finally arrived, and I was going to the mountains with my sister for a short get away. All my bags were packed and now I had to just get ready to prepare my thoughts to go back into my house. I opened the car door and slowly stepped outside the car. The grass felt good under my feet as they began to sink down into the grass. I stood there for a minute, for it felt like fear was being pulled away from me down through my feet

All visions of the skeletal like hands that were pulling me down into the ground begin to disappear as I became grounded by the earth. Grounding with the earth was a technique in which I learnt from my sister as well. She told me that at times we needed to become grounded with *Mother Earth* to be able to pull our energy back in. I walked slowly towards the front door becoming more confident which each step that I was taking. I was not afraid to go inside my home, but I was nervous about there being left over residue from the night before.

I walked into the kitchen and the table was back into its proper place. I saw no evidence of any broken glass either. It was as if last night never happened and everything was normal. Maybe it was all a dream after all. But how in the hell did I end up in my car sleeping?

I walked into my bedroom and my cell phone began ringing. "Hello" I said answering the phone.

"What's up sis?" my sister asked me. "I was sleeping when you called me."

"Nothing much Abenaa. I ended up sleeping in my car," I answered her.

"You had another one of those dreams again?" she asked me.

"Yes, but this time I did not get saved by the Ancestors."

"What happened?" she asked worriedly.

I began telling Abenaa about my dream hoping that she could offer me some assistance. Abenaa was good at dream interpretations. She was also good with Astrology and doing readings. She was not able to see spirits as I did, but she was very in tune with her spirituality and other cultural sciences.

"Before we get on the road let me throw the cards down."

"Abenaa you know how I feel about readings from you," I said to her. "But this time I need some clarification."

"Great," she said happily. "I will be there shortly and make sure you have all your bags pack."

I started laughing. "They were packed yesterday ha-ha!"

Chapter 2

Kente

Kente ran as fast as she could down the hill towards the river. The blood was flowing from the wound on her head and into her eyes. Her village had been attacked by the tribe from the village from the west. She had overheard her mother telling her brother to be careful of them for they were taking others and giving them to the white strangers.

One of the warriors, who was chasing her, had threw a rock at her hitting her in the head. Kente kept running away from the violence that had befallen her village. Kente had been gathering herbs for her mother when the attack took place. She had not even strayed too far away from her mother's hut when she heard the drums alarming them that they were under attack.

Just as she turned her head around, the warrior had thrown a net over her head and she fell to the ground screaming. She tried her best to fight them off, but they were too strong. All she wanted to do was get back to her mother. She was dragged back towards a huge clearing where she saw strange men standing. She was only fifteen and had no idea where she was and where her family could be. She was taken from her village by the warriors from the next tribe, and then they had exchanged her to the white men on horses who carted her off with other girls from her village to a large boat.

She had never seen a boat this big before and she was made to go down into its belly in chains and shackles. She lived in that belly for months with the other girls who also saw no way of escaping this journey.

Kente was hearing others speak about those who were jumping overboard trying to go back home. Some of the girls would be snatched up during the night and taken to the top where she could hear their screams from their rapes and brutality.

Kente's mother had sent her out into the land to search for herbs and berries to help make the magic to cure the sick in the village. Her mother was the high priestess of the village and she had inherited her mother's gift. All the spirits that she called upon could not help her from being taken and she was confused as well as angry.

She was taught that *Ogun* would protect her, and that *Shango* would fight for her but where were they now? They did not stop her captivity and here she was on a boat being taken away from her family.

The men never took her away at night on top of the ship. They had never seen her *kind* with so much beauty. Kente's skin was ebony, but her hair was white flowing down her back like silk. Her almond shaped eyes shown its innocence and her full lips was inviting to even the elders of men.

The white men knew that they would get top money for her, so they chose not to rape her. She was different. Even the other captives stayed away from her because they knew that she possessed special powers and that she was from the spirits world.

The boat had finally stopped moving and Kente was taken on shore to a different land that she did not know. The things that her eyes beheld frightened her, and she was scared that she was going to die. Kente saw her people being branded and whipped. They took her and the girls that were left inside a small house; stripping them of their clothes, they poured buckets of cold water on them. But the scent of those who had died around her did not wash off of her.

They led her and the others onto a platform while others watched. She saw these strange men smiling at her and she felt even more afraid. Kente and the girls were naked, and the men touched and probed their bodies as if they were inspecting livestock. She had never felt more ashamed nor frightened in her life.

As she watched the crowd, she noticed a man eyeing her. He was tall and had hair on his face. But there was something about his eyes which told her that he would not hurt her, and she hoped that she would go to him. As if something had heard her silent prayer, he had outbid the others.

Kente was led off the platform and handed over to the man.

"We can brand her for you," the overseer said to him.

"No need for that," he said to him. He took Kente by the hand and helped her into the back of his cart He handed her some clothes as they rode away.

She did not understand his language, but she knew that the clothes were meant for her. She put them on and silently watched the scenes unfold before her eyes. she was seeing very tall trees and white people watching her in disgust as well as awe. No one had seen a slave look like her before and they were amazed at her beauty as well.

The man who had bought her was also amazed at how beautiful she was to have dark skin. He had out bided all the other slave owners at the auction. For some reason he felt drawn to her. Not just because of her beauty but there was something deep hidden in her eyes and he knew that he had to have her.

He had over 100 slaves on his plantation down in Savannah Georgia and to him he thought of himself as being a good slave master. He allowed his slaves to sing, dance and some could even read. He also allowed them to practice their voodoo in the darkness of their cabins. He would creep up at night and listen to the beating of the makeshift drums and see the women spinning and gyrating as their spirits would come down and possess them.

The moment James had seen Kente he knew that she was of that dark power. He paid close attention to how the other slaves would move away from her as if she would curse them. He was there to buy ten more slaves, but he had used up all his cash to buy her. She had cost him over three hundred dollars. With the amount that he had spent on her, James was not about to put her in the fields.

Kente was so tired, she allowed her body to collapse in the back of the cart. It felt good to her to be able to breathe fresh air and embrace the warmness of the sun. In her homeland the heat was not this dry, but it felt good on her skin. For a moment in her young life she felt relaxed. She closed her eyes and fell asleep.

James looked backed over his shoulder and saw her sleeping. She looked so innocent and he found himself wanting to protect her from *his* world. He could never imagine the pain that she was feeling. He could only imagine the life that he was going to give her at the plantation.

James pulled up in front of his home and his house slaves were all standing outside waiting on him to arrive. They moved closer to the wagon with anticipation of removing slaves, but when they investigated the cart all they saw was the young African girl.

'Master," Jacob said. "Where de slaves at?

James look at him and smiled. He knew that they would be wondering why he had only returned home with one slave.

"Jacob, I decided to buy just this one." James answered, jumping down from the cart.

Mae the big mamma of the house walked over and peered into the cart.

"Lordy Master, you don brought a witch here!" she exclaimed.

"She is not a witch," James replied.

"Massa look at her hair and her skin. Her skin black like mines but her hair ain't normal. She is a witch for sure."

James looked back at Kente laying in the cart. He knew that the others would fear her just as the ones who had shied away from her back at the auction.

"I know she looks different than the rest of you, but I bought her, and I want each one of you to treat her like she is family. She

has had a long trip from Africa, and she is very afraid and nervous.

She does not yet understand our tongue so I will need for you Mae to

teach her our language."

Mae glared up at James with disgust in her eyes. She could

sense that the only reason he had bought her was because she was

beautiful. Mae was from the Congo and she knew that the girl

possessed special magic. It was true the girl was tired because she

slept through their commotion, but Mae did not want anything to

happen to her closeness with James.

Mae was the priestess on the plantation, and she would be

damn if she allowed another to come and take her place. She knew

that by the girl having white hair that she was from a very powerful

tribe up in the mountains and she knew that when that girl hit sixteen

that she was going to be stronger than she could ever be.

As if Jacob could read her thoughts and he could, he spoke to

Mae.

"Mae don have no fear of this child. Instead of ya thinking

she gonna take your place, teach her and show her the right way to use her gift. I know what you done seen it and I done seen it to. We can use her gift to gain our freedom."

Mae looked at Jacob. "Yes, I know but she real, this chile here real and all that come from her will be just as strong and real also."

Chapter 3

Kodia

My sister pulled up in my driveway smiling at me the whole

time. She was perky and she believed that everyone should be perky,

and love like she loved. I used to be so envious of my sister for she

was what we black folk called high yellow. She had the long flowing

red hair and she was often mistaken for a white woman. But when

you looked at her dark eyes and she opened her sassy mouth you

knew that she was indeed a black woman. Not to say black woman

are sassy, but do not piss one off, especially my sister.

Abenaa cut the car off and walked up to the porch to see her

sister. She loved her sister so much. She was very envious of her

sister because she was dark, a beautiful ebony sister the brothers

would call her. She had long flowing white hair and others would

always be amazed at her erotic beauty. People would often accuse

Kodia of coloring her hair, but she was born with white hair. Her

mother had told them before she died that the blood which ran through their veins was strong and powerful.

I often wondered what she meant, but my mother would tell me not to dwell on our past heritage but to keep looking forward to a glorious future which laid ahead of us both. I knew that she was hiding something from me, but I let it go. The secret of my past now laid in an ivory casket ten feet deep beneath the earth.

Abenaa stepped up on my porch with her Ouija board duffel bag and her red candle.

"Are you ready Kodia? " she asked me.

I sighed, "Yeah let's get this over with."

She grabbed my hand and I followed her into my house.

"It's really some crazy energy in here," Abenaa said sitting on the floor of my living room.

"I told you I have been having some crazy dreams."

"I am feeling a lot of shit right now."

"I know sis, Last night was crazy for me."

"Well let's get this reading over so that we can get a start on this drive," she said pulling me down beside her.

My sister reached into her bag and pulled out her small straw mat. She unfolds it and took a red cloth holding her cards, out the bag as well. She loved using playing cards because she said that they are easier to read. Abenaa also told me that they are the original tarot anyway. She handed them to me and told me to hold them in my hands and focus on my wants and desires. I took the cards from her and I closed my eyes concentrating on what I wanted. The answer to my dreams.

I handed her back the cards and she began speaking to the spirits calling out their names while asking them to come and reveal to her what was going on with me. She asked for the owner of the doorways to come and open the doors so that the spirits may pass through.

"*Mafarefun Elegba*, come carry a message to the others to tell them we need them."

As she kept reciting that chant I, could feel myself becoming lightheaded and I knew that they had entered my home from the next realm. I felt a cool breeze brush against me, and I jumped.

"Relax," she spoke softly to me. "Allow them to come in and speak with you. I know you do not really trust all this, but just relax."

I closed my eyes and began to relax. I could hear her dropping the cards on the mat. I opened my eyes and she picked them back up and asked me to cut them in three piles. Abenaa then began turning them over. I notice that the *King of Diamonds* and the *King of Hearts* fell together along with the *Jack of Hearts*. Behind those, the *Ace of Spades* and the *Seven of Clubs* fell behind them, and then fell the *Queen* and *King of Spades*.

She gazed at the cards a few seconds then she began speaking to me.

"The *Kind of Diamonds* and the *King of Hearts* falling together means that you will meet a man who will love you with all his heart. He will have a lot of influence over you and he will want to control you. But you must be careful of him doing things behind your back. Also, this means that he will be either white or very light skin. The *Ace of Spades* means that you will be warring with your emotions and that death is around you. It speaks about bad energy and depression. It warns of bad luck coming your way. You need to pay attention to this card. Also, the *Seven of Clubs* means that you must be careful of trouble coming from the opposite sex. You must be careful of unfaithfulness, but things will be successful and prosperous.

"Well I know that it isn't true for I am not involved with anyone," I said.

"It does not necessarily mean that it could be a man, It could be anyone," she said becoming agitated with me. She continued with the reading. " Now the *King* and *Queen of Spades* means that you have some strong spirits around you. Kodia the spirits of the dead walk strongly with you. it looks like they have been with you for a very long time and they are calling you. You are standing between two worlds, one of the living and one of which belongs to the dead. That can explain the dream of being pulled into the earth with the skeletal hands."

I looked at her in awe. "This is so crazy!"

She smiled at me. "Yes, but my readings are telling you what is coming. Their energy may change but some of it will come to pass."

"Well I do not know about the white or light skin guy because I like my men dark, but those spirits that are with me didn't save my ass in my dream."

"Kodia," Abenaa said shaking her head." Your dreams have a deeper meaning. what I am getting from them is that the dead walks with you and you are being called to work with them."

I shook my head at her as well. "I know something is going on. I just want this to stop so that I can get rid of the bags under my eyes."

"Well sis once we get to the mountains and breathe in that fresh air, hopefully you will be able to get plenty of rest. Besides I will be there casting a spell over you so you can sleep."

I laughed then sighed. "I hope that you are right. Let's go!"

I stood up and waited for my sister to gather her things together. As I closed the door behind me, walking out the house, I hoped that she was right.

Chapter 4

Kente

Kente began opening her eyes slowly. She blinked them several times trying to allow them to get use the light. Jacob was sitting beside her cot watching her. She rubbed her eyes and sat up. She looked down on the floor and saw Jacob sitting there. She scurried closer to the top of the cot in fear.

"Do not be afraid child. I know that you may not understand my voice, but you are safe and in good company," Jacob said to her.

Kente did not understand English for she only knew her native tongue, but she sensed that the big black man would not hurt her. Jacob pointed his finger to his chest.

"Jacob," he spoke softly.

Kente looked at him.

"Jacob," he repeated.

Kente realized that he was telling her what his name was. She pointed at her chest.

"Kente".

Jacob smiled. Kente was a fast learner and he knew that in no time she would learn how to speak the white man's language just as he had done many years ago.

Kente watched Jacob staring at her. She was not afraid of the big man, but she was nervous for she did not know what was going to happen to her. She could feel his spirit and to her it felt free and good. While others had been taught in her village to do this, it came naturally to her to be able to see into other people souls.

"Kente I am going to go fetch you some water so that you may wash ya' self and put on some mo' clothes."

Kente nodded her head. She really did understand him this time. It was as if the spirits were whispering in her ears translating his language to her.

As soon as Jacob left the room, in walked the darkest and smallest woman that Kente had ever seen. The dark woman watched her carefully as Kente allowed her eyes only to follow the woman around the woman.

Mae walked around the room slowly never taking her eyes

from her. This girl was more powerful than she would ever be. She knew that when she came into her own the others would swarm around her like bees to honey. She was very envious of Kente already because she could see how Master had looked at her. She was the head woman in charge, and she was not like going to allow this child to grow up and take her place.

Kente could read Mae's thoughts. She did not want to be in charge. All she wanted to do was go back across the water to her home and see her mother's face once more. She did know that she was special and that others from her village had told her that she had been born with spirits by her side, but she was also told that she once she turned sixteen, that all would come to her and she would be high priestess.

All Kente wanted to do was to play with the other girls and dance around the fire. Her mother told her that it would never be allowed for she had to learn the ways of the spirits and how to mix the herbs to heal others and counsel the chief when the time would arise. Kente was an obedient child, so she listened carefully to her mother as she learned the ways of the herbs and how to speak with

the spirits. They were her friends, yet they had failed her and

allowed her to be taken from her village and brought to this place

that she nor her forefathers had ever known. What was the use of all

that training?

Mae watched Kente watching her and walked over to the cot.

She sat down beside her.

"Hmmm you are just a child, but soon you will be a grown

woman."

Kente stared at her.

"You will never be me. I don't care about your magic waiting

to come out. You will never be me!" Mae whispered to her.

Kente stared at her.

"You keep lookin' at me like you have no respect for me but

you will."

Kente stared at her still showing no fear.

Mae grabbed her by the face and pulled her face into hers.

she gazed into her eyes trying to spell her. Kente's eyes turned black like two deep ebony coals and Mae was pushed back against the wall. The whole room shook. Mae stared in fright as Kente's face changed. Kente's eyes rolled to the back of her head as Mae saw her become possessed.

"Mae, we have no problems with you," the spirit spoke to her in her Congo tongue.

"There is no need for you to be jealous of her. If you do stop with all this hate you will die. Teach her and help her and you will be rewarded once she leaves. Despise her and mistreat her and you will die as I snatch your soul from your body."

Mae grabbed her chest and shook her head yes in understanding.

Kente was released by the spirit and fell back on the bed.

Just as she fell back on the bed, Jacob entered the room. He saw Mae against the wall holding her chest and Kente laying on the bed as if she was lifeless.

"Kente," he yelled. "Wake up!"

"She-she is in the spirit," Mae managed to stammer.

"What you do to this gal?" Jacob asked her never taking his eyes off Kente.

"I was trying to speak to her," Mae answered slowly.

Jacob shook his head in distrust at Mae. "I do not believe you."

Mae knew that Jacob had caught her in a lie. She was scared and she knew that the spirit that possessed Kente meant what she said. Jealousy is an emotion that will eat you up until it killed you. She was frightened for now, but she was not going to allow Kente to get the best of her.

"Mae we must help this girl. She is far away from her home and she needs someone in her life that she can count on. We got to band together so that we can free ourselves from being slaves. Maybe not so much as now because we have freedom when we worship our spirits."

Mae knew that Jacob was right. "I agree."

Jacob looked at Kente laying there. He had brought her some water with lemongrass weed in it to drink. He placed the tin cup beside the small bed and rubbed her face.

"We going to leave you be." he glanced at Mae. "Let her rest."

Mae followed Jacob out of the room, but she never took her eyes off Kente. This was far from over.

Kente opened her eyes as soon as she heard the door close behind them. Whatever had possessed her had given her strength and she was not scared anymore. It left her with a gift to be able to speak and understand their language. The spirit that was inside her told her she had been female, and she had made her stronger. In a matter of minutes Kente had matured and she had read Mae's mind. Mae was going to be trouble, but the spirit had told her that she would protect her. Kente picked up the small tin cup that Jacob had left for her and took a sip. It was bittersweet to her taste, but it was soothing. She took off her clothes and poured the lemon water over her body. She was purging her soul and cleansing all that energy from her journey to that strange land. She laid back on the bed and as she allowed the cool air to caress her, she drifted back off to sleep and dreamed of her mother teaching her.

James stood in the window watching Kente as she slept. She was beautiful to him. He had laid down with plenty of his female slaves, but Kente was different and he was intrigued by her beauty. He allowed his hand to caress himself as he released while watching her sleep.

Chapter 5

Kodia

The mountains were beautiful this time of year. I am so glad that my sister suggested that we take this trip. I needed to breathe in the fresh air and really get myself in tune with nature. We had taken I40 past Winston -Salem and we were approaching Asheville. I love that city so I asked my sister to get off in Asheville so that I could do a little shopping at some of the small shops that they had there.

Asheville was known for its rich culture as well as its different diversity of people who flocked to her warmth year after year. It was nothing to see the natives walking around in tie dye shirts and having all kinds of festivals during the summer. That's not even including the Biltmore House with all her richness.

We got off at the first exit that we saw, and it took us straight into the heart of Asheville. We parked in the first parking deck that we spotted and got out and started walking.

"I love this place," I said to my sister happily.

"Me too. I want to move here," she replied back.

"Yeah this city is all you with the crystals and all that shit you are into."

Abenaa laughed, "Yeah you are into it too, but you do not know it!"

I shook my head at her. It was true that I was intrigued by all this new age shit, but I was not into it as she was. My mother used to tell us stories about our Ancestors and how spiritual we were. She said that our great ancestral grandmother was very powerful and that she walked strongly with the spirits of the dead. I didn't want to hear those stories. Especially the ones she told about how they were slaves. I really did not believe in all that spooky shit. But there was something going on with me that was scaring the shit out of me.

As we started walking, we notice that there was some type of pagan festival going on. Crowds of people were walking around in Medieval costumes. I saw a man walking around in all black with an owl resting on his shoulder. Nearby there were little girls wearing fairy wings and all kinds of booths set up with people selling merchandise. Immediately Abenaa's eyes lit up and she was ready to start blending in. She spotted a few sisters at a booth who were doing rituals with water.

"Kodia, let's go over there."

I looked at the sisters at their booth and all three of them look like enchantresses with all their darkness and colorful beads. I did not want to walk over there but before I could protest, she was dragging me behind her.

We approached the table and stood back a few feet waiting for their ritual to end. They had a huge copper bowl in the middle of the table filled with water and there were all these herbs floating around. I saw a beautiful statue of a black woman with a fish tail. She was very pretty, and I liked seeing the black mermaid image. Beside her was this statue of a black woman covered in yellow with long flowing hair as well and she appeared to be holding a honey pot. Beside her was a statue of a black female warrior. She was beautiful and magnificent with long flowing white hair. She had on a red scarf which covered her breasts and there were skulls all around her feet. The color of her hair was white like mines and her face resembled mines as well. I could not take my eyes off her as I watched her. She was moving towards me and I felt myself being drawn to her. I started walking slowly to her and I could feel my feet slightly rising off the ground under my long skirt. I could hear her voice and she was calling me.

Abenaa grabbed me and it broke me out of my trance.

"You okay?" she asked me.

"Yes-s-s," I stammered.

"Are you sure because I was just talking to you and you were not answering me."

I looked at her and then back at the table. We were still standing a few feet away from their booth.

"What were you asking me?"

"I was *telling* you that they were done, and we could move closer to check out their stuff they had for sale."

"Oh ok," I replied.

She grabbed my hand and we walked closer to their table.

As soon as we approached the shelter of their tent the three sisters both gasped and fell to their knees as if they were prostrating themselves before me.

"*Mama Kente, Mama Kente* ," they chanted in unison.

I began to become nervous from the sound of that name.

The sisters raise their head and looked directly at me, repeating that name *Kente.*

I did not know why they were calling me that. It was scaring me, and I started backing up from their booth. My sister grabbed my arm and began pulling me towards her.

"Mama," one of the sisters said." you have returned back to us"

"I am not your mama and I do not know what in the hell you are talking about," I said my voice trembling. The sisters looked at me as if I had just spoken a curse at me.

"You have returned to us. We worship you."

I held on to my sister and we turned around and ran back towards the car. I was so fearful of what those women were talking about. Not only that but something had taken hold of me when we were at their booth and it had me shaken up.

"What in the hell was that about?" I asked my sister.

"Sis I do not know," Abenaa answered nervously.

"Why you do not know?" I exclaimed. "You are the one that is into all this hocus pocus bull shit!"

"Look Kodia," she said angrily. "I really do not know. I have never heard of a spirit named *Kente*. Apparently, she is their goddess and they feel that you are her."

"I am sorry for yelling at you," I said calming down. "But when we were there it was like that statue of that warrior female came alive and it had me in a trance. It was calling me, and I felt like I was connected to her."

"That explains why you looked spaced out."

"You know I think that we should get back on the highway and keep it moving. I do not know what is going on here, but I do not like it."

"For once sis ," my sister said, "I am in agreement."

As we walked back towards the parking deck where the car was located, I glanced back over my shoulders, for it felt like someone was following us. I began walking faster to reach the car. We got back into the car and drove until we saw the sign leading us back to I40. I did not like being called by that name. But at the same time, once the fear left it felt like I could have been her. It felt as if she had entered me from that statue and that she was trying to be a part of me. Something is going on here and I know that I did not want it to overtake my life.

Abenaa looked over at her sister. She hated lying to her, but she did know who *Kente* was. *Kente* was their great ancestor who had been a powerful voodoo Mambo. She was even more powerful than Marie Laveau. Her mother had told her the stories of *Kente*, but never had disclosed that information to Kodia. Abenaa was jealous of Kodia because she looked just like *Kente*. She also knew that *Kente* was inside of her sister and she had to protect Kodia from the bullshit of fake followers. Her mother had told her that she had to take her to the mountains to have her take the rites of passage to become fully engulfed with *Kente's* power. She hoped that when

Kodia discovers the true nature of their trip, she would forgive her

for lying. Those sisters had almost fucked things up for her, but it

had given her additional confirmation that *Kente* is Kodia

reincarnated.

Chapter 6

Kente

Kente woke up with the sun the next morning. Slowly she got up from the small cot and stretched. She began giving thanks to the ancestors for her new day and then she felt her stomach growling. She walked towards the door and slowly opened it. She stood on the porch embracing nature. Even though she was not in her homeland she still respected nature. She raised her hands high above her hand and let out a yell. She looked up over her head and there were nine crows flying over her head. She knew that the spirits were with her by giving her a sign with those black birds.

There were several other small houses like hers and she imagined that others lived in those houses. She saw a path leading through the woods and she began walking towards it. She felt like it was her own personal path and she had to see where it would take her. She kept walking until she came to a clearing in the shape of a circle. There was a huge stone in the middle of that circle, and she went and sat on it. The morning sun was bright, and she removed all her clothes as she laid back on the rock and allowed the sun rays to enhance her melanin.

She closed her eyes and began doing the breathing ritual her mother had taught her. Kente's mother had taught her how to leave her body and project herself to anyplace she wanted to be. She slowed her breathing down until she could feel herself levitating. She could feel herself separating from her body. Kente glanced down at her physical body lying on the rock and took off flying. She could feel herself flying back to her homeland until she reached her village.

Kente saw her friends doing chores and preparing for the day. She then realized that her village was still intact. She flew on and she saw her father talking to the warriors of the village. She kept going because she was looking for her mother. She arrived at their hut and went in.

"I been waiting on you," her mother said. She was stooped down mixing herbs in a wooden bowl.

"They took me nana," Kente cried. "I thought they had killed you!"

Her mother turned around and saw her daughter standing there. Kente looked at her mother's face and burst into tears. Her mother went to her and embraced her. "They came, but our warriors fought them off. I sent your brother out to search for you, for it seemed like all they wanted was the young women."

"Nana I am scared. I know no one and I am so afraid."

"Do not be afraid of that strange land."

Kente hugged her mother tightly. "I want to come home."

"You can come and visit me when you leave your body. You are there for a reason and know that *Maman* is with you. *They* will protect you. The man with the colorless face will protect you as well."

"What are you talking about " Kente asked her. "*They* did not protect me!"

Her mother released her from her embrace.

"I know that you are young and scared, but *they* will help

you. You will have to prove your power to those who look like you because they fear you and their little magic is just that, little."

Kente was confused. "Why are you telling me this?"

"Because I need you to be strong and not be afraid. You are strong and the dead will help you. You will have many friends as well as many enemies. Your enemies will be of the same color as you so you must ask the spirts to reveal them to you. Some pain you will endure but it will be okay for it is meant. I made you this mixture and once you drink it you will be able to understand more. Not the ones who look like you but the men who have no color. You will also need to be the owner of the nine masks in order to protect your power. "

"Owner of nine masks, what does that it means?"

"You will have to learn how to disguise yourself." She handed the mixture to her.

Kente took the mixture and drunk it slowly. It tasted sweet and bitter at the same time.

"Kente I know that I have said a lot, but I need you to not

worry. You will be all right. I need you to rely solely on your spirit guides and the ancestors. Remember all the herb remedies I have taught you and allow the spirits to show you how to work. You will be prosperous. Use your power for good and only for bad to protect yourself. I love you and know that I am here."

"Nana I want to stay!" Kente cried.

"No Kente," her mother said forcefully. "If you stay out of your body for long periods of time you will die."

Kente looked at her mother and obeyed. Her mother was great in her village and she had told her that she would be okay.

"Okay Nana I will listen and obey. But please tell Baba that I love him and my brother. I will come back soon."

Her mother looked at her and said nothing. She knew that Kente would never come back to her in the physical. She would tell her brother nothing. Not even her father would know that she had visited.

Kente walked over to her mother and hugged her. She began to feel herself flying back to her body and she saw herself laying there on the rock. Slowly she drifted down into herself. She took a huge gasp of air and opened her eyes. Silently she began to cry, and she was grateful that she had went to see her mother.

Kente began putting her clothes on. After she got dressed, she started walking back towards the path. It was as is the trees separated for her and she could see a huge white house. As she moved closer to the house, she saw smoke coming from the chimney. Kente could smell something good being cooked. The grumblings in her belly had reminded her that she was hungry. She was going there to eat.

James had slept outside her house all night. He was in love with the dark beauty and he could not leave her side. He had followed her into the woods, and he watched through the trees as she had undressed herself and laid on the rock. Her body was beautiful. Even though she was a young girl she had beautiful firm dark breasts and her nipples were dark and perfect. The bush between her legs was white like her hair, and it was a perfect V-shape between her legs. He lusted after her. John watched her as she got dressed and tonight, he had decided to take her into his house and bed her.

Kente approached the huge white house and stopped. this place was magnificent to her young eyes. She was anxious to see what was inside this huge house. She slowly began walking up the stairs to the huge porch. The porch was so big that it encircled the whole house. She was mesmerized by the size of it and she kept walking until she reached the front door. She noticed that the front door was slightly ajar, and she went in.

The hardwood floors were shining, and she could see her reflection. She was almost scared to walk on them. The stairs were winding up to the second floor like a huge white albino snake. The scent which had caused her to stomach to ache from hunger was coming from behind those stairs. She walked towards the stairs and she began hearing the faint sound of drums. The hunger pains began to fade as she moved closer to the stairs.

When she arrived at the foot of the first step, she placed her left foot upon it. Slowly she began ascending them. As she took each step, she felt like she was being called, no more like being pulled to walk up those stairs. It was if she was in a trance and she could hear the drums from her village beating in her ears. When she came to the top of the stairs the drums were beating louder and louder. She moved towards the room from where the sound was coming from. Kente pushed opened the door and walked in.

Mae and Jacob were sitting inside a white circle. The circle was made by white flour and they were facing each other. Mae's face was covered in white powder. Her head was thrown back and she was swaying back and forth. Kente glanced to the left of her and saw a small table with food on it. Jacob was beating on the drums and they were unaware that Kente had entered the room.

Kente looked at them and she began swaying like Mae. She felt the room spinning and she began spinning with it. Her body was not her own as she twirled and twirled to the rhythm of the drums. Her arms began to stretch open and she felt this presence enter her small body. Her back began to arch and she welcomed the power that was engulfing her. Suddenly she began to screech and cry out. Her screeching sound brought Mae out of her trance.

Mae came out of her trance and she watched in awe as Kente became possessed with the spirit that she was calling to *her*. For years Mae had been trying to summon *Marinette-Bras Cheche* to come to her and possess her, but she never came. She was a Petro loa, and they were violent and fierce. Mae had been trying to summon her to come and help throw off the shackles of their enslavement. All the other spirits would come to her, but she desired *Marinette* to come more than the others. *Marinette* granted you the power to shape shift into *Lycans*, werewolves.

Marinette was considered a powerful and outstanding sorceress who used the owls as her messenger. She loved all things black and fire. Mae had heard from other slaves who had come for the island of Haiti, that she had once been a woman. There were tales of her summoning *Erzulie Dantor* to help free her people from slavery.

The ritual that she had performed had worked but *Marinette* had been captured. They had told her how she had been burned alive and immediately was taken up by the spirit world and transformed into a loa. Whenever she mounted someone, she would cause them to screech and yell and violence would take place. She was considered as the female aspect of the devil. A truly evil spirit that is totally respected by werewolves.

Mae could not understand why she had chosen Kente as her surrogate. She could not be angry with Kente anymore. She had to bow her head in *Marinette's* presence and accept her as her Voodoo queen.

Kente began to levitate off the floor and hovering over Mae. Jacob was in a trance and he just kept beating the drums sporadically. Mae kept her head bowed in total submission as she felt the power surging form Kente. Kente looked down at Mae and she could feel the spirit inside of her and loved her. *Marinette* loved the feel of the young body that she possessed. This vessel was already called by the dark power that she served, and she had been sent to protect her on this land.

She looked down at Mae in disgust. What was this ugly small black woman could be thinking of? She could never contain my energy nor be this voodoo queen that she wanted to be.

"Mae you will be my servant and do my bidding."

"Yes, my queen," Mae whispered.

"You will have my ceremony in the open in the woods and I want black chickens and goats. I will grant you want you want to be freed from slavery."

Mae smiled; she would do whatever she had to do get her freedom. She would serve the queen but not the girl

"You will serve the both of us. If you come up against her in any way, I will burn your soul."

Mae was stunned. She did not know that *Marinette* had read her mind. She would have to be careful with her thoughts.

Kente began floating slowly down to the floor and coming back to herself. She could still feel her inside of her, but she was more aware of everything surrounding her. The air was different and the sounds from outside were stronger. She was more aware of life. She looked down at Mae and saw her bowing down at her. She touched her on the shoulder and told her to rise.

Slowly Mae arose and keeping her head bowed she, she grabbed Kente's hand and kissed it.

"I will be your faithful servant," she spoke softly.

"I know you will serve her well just as I will," Kente said in the language of her slave master.

Mae raised her head and stared at Kente. She peered into her eyes as if she was still trying to see any traces of *Marinette.* Kente stared backed at her knowing that she was searching for any traces of *Marinette. Marinette* knew it as well and she would keep herself hidden for now, for she knew that a jealous woman could never be trusted

"She is gone," Kente said lying to her.

"I cannot believe that you can speak my tongue," Mae said.

"I guess when she entered me, she opened my understanding of the tongue of these white people." Kente was not going to reveal to her how she knew it. She had to listen to her mother's warning about who would be against her.

Mae was even more jealous of Kente. She knew that she

would have to play it off like she was not envious, but she was. How did she get to be chosen to carry her? *Marinette* was hers and she would not let this child hold that energy for long.

Jacob had come out of his trance and was watching both. He could see that Mae was trying to hide her emotion of jealousy towards the young girl. Kente was chosen by *Marinette* and for that he would protect her from Mae's hate and all others who would try to hurt her.

"Jacob," Mae said to him. "Kente can speak in our tongue."

"Yes, I can see and hear that," Jacob said.

"We will make sure that she is okay and in three nights we will have a ceremony for *Marinette* in the woods under the tent."

Jacob nodded his head in agreement.

"Jacob walk her back to her shack."

"C'mon Kente, let me take ya' back to ya' bed. You need some rest after all that."

Kente looked at Jacob lovingly. For some reason she trusted him more than Mae and she knew that he would always be there for her.

"Yep I am tired," she said to him. "But can we please get some food for I am hungry."

Jacob walked over the small table and grabbed the plate of food and handed it to her.

He wrapped his arms around Kente and walked out the door, down the steps and towards her shack.

Mae walked over to the window and watched them walk away. She hated that white-headed girl and she vowed that she would kill her or die trying. She was the voodoo queen of that plantation and she be damned if a child was going to take her place. She watched as they disappeared down the path into the woods and she stood there plotting her revenge.

Chapter 7

Kodia

Once we got back on I40 , I began to relax a little more. I could not believe that the women were bowing down to me and calling me *Mama Kente*. That statue that was on their altar was a very likeness of myself and I was drawn to it. I still feel residue of it lingering on me. I looked over at my sister and she was holding the steering wheel tightly as if she was angry at me.

"What's wrong with you, "I asked her.

Abenaa cut her eyes at me. "Nothing, just did not like the way those witches were carrying on over you."

I looked at my sister. She said it as if she resented me for how they had behaved.

"Damn you said that like it was my fault," I said to her.

"I didn't mean to say it like that . It's just that we are on a this get away to relax and not get all upset by ignorant people. "

" I do not think that they are ignorant. I think that they just strongly believe in their way of life. Besides you must admit, I did favor that statue with the white hair."

Abenaa tried to keep her emotions from showing in her face. She knew that Kodia was not aware of their great Ancestor. She also knew that she would have to release her jealousy of her sister in order to be able to help her embrace all *Kente's* energy. "Yeah that was just a coincidence."

I glanced down at my hands and began rubbing them. Whenever my sister was lying my hands would start aching. I was going to let this slide for now, because I knew that soon I would know the truth about what had occurred at that festival.

My sister pulled down the sun visor and I saw she had her CDs already staged there. She grabbed a green cd and I knew that it was Jhene Aiko. She knew that I loved her as well and she placed it in the disk holder. As Jhene began singing I turned my head and started enjoying the view of the mountains.

We were heading towards the Great Smoky Mountains , moving closer to Knoxville

I looked down into the valley and I could see small houses and green meadows. It looked so peaceful and so quiet. I began to wonder what life was like for those people who lived there.

I looked up ahead and I saw a sign that said Lake Junaluska, Hot Springs exit 24.

"We are almost there, " Abenaa said to me.

We kept driving and got off at exit 24.

Chapter 8

James

James sat in his parlor listening to the drumming noise coming from upstairs. He saw Kente when she went inside, and he went into his parlor. He did not care what Mae and Jacob was doing in his house. He was gentle to his slaves and Mae and Jacob kept everyone in line. He liked the music from the drums for it soothed his soul and he was able to think and relax while they played and beat and beat. At times he felt as if it was his own heart, he could feel it beating in rhythm with those drums.

He heard the drums stop when he heard a screeching sound. It sounded like Kente and he rushed upstairs to make sure that she wasn't hurt. He dares not open the door being afraid of what he might see . He placed his ears to the door, and he could hear laughter and a woman speaking that did not sound like Mae nor Kente's voice.

Slowly he cracked open the door and saw Kente floating off the floor and moving towards Mae. Mae was lying flat on the floor prostrating herself to Mae and he had never seen her so humble.

James moved his eyes over to Kente and she looked more beautiful than he could ever imagine. Her face was glowing, and her white hair was longer and floating way down her back. Her eyes were blazing bright and her body was fuller and womanly. He closed the door behind him and crept back downstairs.

This was not his thing, but he had been drawn to it. James knew that he could never interfere like the other owners did with their slaves. He wanted them all to be free and he hated this inhuman act of owning slaves. He had inherited this plantation from his father. His mother had died giving birth to him. He had been the only child and all his father's wealth belonged to him.

There had been many slave women whom his father ad slept with, but his father had been unable to produce any seed with any of them. He believed that Mae had placed juju on the women to not bear children for the white man. This had to be true for all the slave women had had slept with, none had given him a child yet.

His father had sent him away to be educated and learn the

way of the land. He knew how to harvest the crops that he grew there, and he loved educating his workers. Yet they were not free. So, he gave them freedom as much as he could give by allowing them to practice their old ways.

As he sat in the chair in his parlor, he had decided that he wanted Kente to be his wife. He did not find any white woman attractive. He did not hate the woman of his race, but he longed for the exotic beauty of the darker skin. James wanted something different in his life and he chose to not want a white woman as his wife.

James heard footsteps coming down the stairs and he moved quietly to the door to see who it was. He watched as Jacob and Kente came down the stairs and walked out the front door. His thoughts still raced in his mind that tonight he was going to take her and make her his wife.

Chapter 9

Kodia

I could not believe how beautiful Lake Junaluska was. The meaning of its name is *"the lake which meets the mountains"*. It was picture perfect! The lake was huge, and it seemed as if the mountains protected it from the outside world. Of course, it was a tourist attraction, but nature was still intact.

Abenaa told me that she had rented us a secluded cottage away from others and I was thankful for that. She told me that the cottage was called the *"Myers Cottage"* and that it was found North 43 Simplicity Way.

When we arrived at the cottage it was indeed secluded and incredibly beautiful. We still had a view of the lake and the mountains. We were located on the Northside of the lake away from people. The cottage was white, small and quaint. It had two bedrooms, but of course there was room to sleep at least six people. It was a single-story cottage with a deck that encircled the whole cottage. The deck reminded me of the porch from my dreams which encircled the white house that I kept running to.

I was in a rush to get inside to take a closer look. "Hurry up and open the door," I said anxiously to my sister.

"Stop rushing me," she said becoming annoyed. Abenaa turned the key in the lock and the door popped open as if someone had been standing on the other side.

The living room was humbly furnished with a sofa bed and two armchairs. It opened into a dining room area with a wooden table and 4 wooden chairs. There was a round multicolored woven rug in the center of the room. Hanging from the lofty ceilings was a chandelier made of deer horns. There was a deer head fixed over the fireplace.

I walked into the kitchen and opened all the cabinets. We had dishes and pots as well as cooking utensils. There were spices left in the cupboard and lots of coffee and hot chocolate. The two bedrooms had their own full bathroom which was great for us. My sister can be a bit messy at times.

The sun was setting and as I walked outside to gather my

bags, I could see the real beauty of nature. The red and orange hues from the sun rays were casting a purplish glow in the sky and I felt as if I was at home. It felt as if this was the place for me. I took a deep breath inhaling the fresh air and walked inside. I could hear the shower running so I knew that my sister would go to bed early. She was tired from doing all the driving so I would let her rest until the morning.

I walked back outside and sat in the rocking chair on the porch. It was still hot, but I could feel a cool breeze blowing against my face. As the breeze blew across my face, I began to smell cinnamon.

I closed my eyes as I laid my head back against the chair and drifted off to sleep.

I am in a bed laying naked and searching for a blanket to cover me. I can hear footsteps outside my door and then slowly the door opens. I see him the white man, tall dark and handsome. He begins walking towards me and I cannot move. I can hear whisperings in my ear telling me to allow him to come closer. He removes all his clothes and lie next to me. He asks me if he can touch me and I shake my head yes giving him permission. He slowly caresses my body and his hands feel gentle and warm. He traces his finger around my breasts and touches my nipples. I am nervous but no more frightened. He begins to kiss me softly and he takes one of my nipples into his mouth. I tense up but the more he sucks the less tense I become. He speaks to telling me that he would never hurt me and that I belonged to him. He tells me that he knows that I am young, but I will be his wife and that he will not allow me to endure the hardships of slavery. I hear a woman's voice whispering in my ear to accept him, I open my legs and he gets between them. He touches me in the soft place, and he can feel my wetness. Slowly he guides his penis inside of me and I feel no pain. He moves in rhythm to my heartbeat and I feel safer than I have ever felt in my life. When it is over, he whispers in my ear, "I love you Kente." I open my eyes.

I see this man out of my dreams standing over me and I fall back out of the chair and hit the window. I look back up and the man is not there. I hear Abenaa running from her room and she gets to me.

"Kodia are you okay," she asks me.

"Yes;" I answered. She helps me up and I began looking around the yard. "Did you see him?" I ask her.

"See who?" my sister says looking around as well.

"There was a man standing over me. I must have dozed off and when I opened my eyes he was standing right here."

"Sis no one is here but us. I saw no one. I heard a loud noise hit the window and I rushed to your room. When I did not see you, I ran outside and saw you laying here."

I looked at my sister like she was crazy. I knew that I had been dreaming, but the man was real, and he looked like the man in my dreams.

"Let's go in the house," my sister said taking my hand and guiding me inside. She led me to the sofa and brought me a bottle of alkaline water to drink. She sat down beside me on the sofa.

"Did you dream?" she asks me.

"Yes," I answered her. "But guess what ?"

"What?"

I dreamt that I was losing my virginity to this white man and he called me *Kente* like those witches did in Asheville."

"Girl you are tired. It's been a long day for you. Go take a shower and get some rest. I will lock up."

I could not believe how my sister just brushed me off like that. But she was right. I got up and walked into my room to take a shower.

Abenaa went to the front door to lock it. She peeked out the window and saw a huge white owl sitting in the tree. She glanced down on the ground and saw footsteps leading into the woods.

Chapter 10

William

I had just arrived in Asheville and had gotten a room at the Marriott. I had been on my way to Knoxville to put up cameras at this storage space facility. I had been driving from Virginia Beach all night and I was tired. I did not have to be at the job site until 9:30 am, so I had decided to stop.

The desk clerk told me that there was a pagan festival going on downtown, so she was shocked that I had been able to book a room. She handed me the room key which was on the 9th floor, Room 921. I smirked at myself. For some reason, I keep seeing the number nine pop up. I placed my bags on the bed and jumped into the shower.

Walking outside I decided to go downtown to the festival. The clerk had told me that there would be food trucks there. I loved food trucks and I wanted to eat something different besides pizza. Luckily for me, my hotel was not too far away, and I had only to walk a couple of blocks.

I began walking towards the smells from the food trucks when these two gorgeous black girls had stepped off the elevator from the parking deck. I fell back so that I could see which direction they would heading in. The women were both gorgeous but the one with the white hair was beyond beautiful. The way her hair cascaded down her back and surrounded her face made her look like an angel. Her skin tone was smooth and ebony, and she had deep dimples when she smiled.

I staid back a few feet from them as I followed them. I wanted to approach her, but would she even talk to a white guy like me? She looked as if she was only into black guys and would never date outside her race. That would be a risk that I would have to take, for I wanted this woman. I could feel my manhood jump in my pants as my desire for her began to rise.

I watched them as they approached a booth where three witches stood. They were beautiful as well.

"Damn, North Carolina got some beautiful women," I thought to myself.

The three witches began bowing down in front of the one with the white hair and I could sense that she was becoming edgy and nervous. I wanted to run to protect her, but I could not move. It felt as if I had been planted in the ground to watch this scene unfold.

The three witches began chanting and really acting weird. I watched as the one with the white hair yelled back at them that she was not who they thought she was. I could hear them calling her *Kente.* That name was beautiful. The woman that was with the one with the white hair, grabbed her by the arm and pulled her away. At that moment my legs were released, and I was able to walk again.

Hurriedly I followed them in the direction from where they I had first seen them. The one with the white hair turned back around as if to see if they were following them. I ducked behind the side of building barely missing her from seeing me. I could see the color of her eyes and they were just as beautiful as she was. She turned back around, and I began following them again.

I watched them as they got into their car, a red Infiniti and started it. I could not let her escape me. Quickly I ran back to the hotel and to my truck. I opened the door and sped out the deck. I could not allow them to get to far ahead of me or I would never find them.

I drove past the parking deck where they had been. I saw the back of their car make a right at the light and head towards I40. They were driving in the same direction that I needed to go, towards Tennessee. I arrived at the light and made a right turn as well. Luckily for me this was a hilly place, for I saw them on the highway. I never took my eyes off that red car.

I followed them all the way to the lake. The lake was gorgeous, but I did not have time to admire its beauty. I parked my truck a few feet away from their cottage as I observed them walking inside. Why I was out here acting like a damn stalker? What the hell was wrong with me?

I took a seat on the ground as I waited until I get up the nerve to knock on the door and approach her. Finally, I saw the door opened and *she* walked out. I watched her as she went and sat down in the rocking chair. She looked very relaxed and I knew that this would be the perfect time for me to walk up and introduce myself.

Slowly I moved towards her, and I noticed that she had fallen asleep. With ease, I stepped on to the porch and moved quietly towards her. She looked like a beautiful angel sleeping in that chair. I suddenly had the urge to whisper in her ear and tell her that I loved her. Just as I was about to lean down, she opened her eyes and I startled her. She fell back against the window and I jumped off the porch and ran towards the woods.

After I felt like she had not followed me nor seen me, I moved back close enough to be able to hear the conversation between her and the other woman. I stared at them both seeing similarities in their looks. The other woman was exceptionally light with red hair and could easily pass for white, but they had the same mouth. They were sisters. The one with the red hair had called out her name *Kodia*, which will stay with me forever.

I got back in my truck and drove back to the hotel. I was going to waste that money on that room for I was going back to where she was and sleep in my truck.

Chapter 11

Kente

As Kente laid on my cot, she heard a gentle knock at the door. She thought it was Jacob and she told him to come in. To her surprise it was James the white man who had bought and brought me here. She watched him as he lowered his head to enter her tiny dwelling. His hair was the color of dark bamboo and he had facial hair. His eyes were the color of emeralds as he stared back at me. He acted as if he was nervous to approach her.

Kente sat up in the cot and pulled the blanket around herself. She was not wearing clothes and her dress was hanging over the wooden chair. James walked over Kente and sat on the cot. He held his head down as he spoke.

"How are you Kente?" he asked her.

"I am good considering where I am," she said to him.

"I know this is all new to you, and I dare to think how that awful voyage was," he spoke softly to her.

Kente stared at him.

"Do you mind if I lay beside you?" he asked her.

"You are my owner, and this is your place. You can do what you want," she answered.

James looked at her in awe. How could this young girl speak his language so fluently? It was as if she had been born in this country. Her voice was so sweet, so mature.

Kente could feel *Marinette* rising in her and she needed her to come thru and save her from what this man was about to do. She remembered what her mother ad told her abut the man, and she tried to appear calm and show no fear. She watched as James took of his clothes and laid beside her. He asked her if he can touch her and she shook her head yes giving him permission. He slowly caresses her body and his hands feel gentle and warm. He traces his finger around her breasts and touches her nipples. Kente is nervous but no more frightened. He begins to kiss her softly and he takes one of her nipples into his mouth. Kente tense's up but the more he sucks the less nervous she becomes. He speaks to her telling Kente that he would never hurt her and that she belonged to him. He tells her that he knows that she is young, but she will be his wife and that he will not allow her to endure the hardships of slavery. Kente hear *Marinette's* voice whispering in my ear to accept him. She opens her legs and he get between them. He touches her in her soft place, and he can feel her wetness. Slowly he guides his penis inside of her and she feels no pain. He moves in rhythm to her heartbeat as it beats faster, and Kente begins to feel safer than she has since coming to the strange land.

When it is over, he whispers in her ear, "I love you Kente."

Kente wraps her arms around his neck holding him close to her. Maybe it was the need to want to be loved, from being taken away from her family, but she needed this. She remembers her mother telling her that this man would help her. As she removed her arms from around him tears began to flow from her eyes.

"Are you okay?' he asked her to sit up on the cot.

"Yes."

"I hope I was not too much for you. I would never want to hurt a hair on your head."

Kente covered her face with her hands and wept into them.

"I cannot take this seeing you cry like this."

She kept her face covered for she knew that one day she would experience this, but she thought that it would be with one from her village. Kente refused to uncover her face.

James got up and began putting his clothes back.

"Tomorrow you will move into *my* house with me. I need to know that you are somewhere safe, and I want you to lay on soft mattresses and not need for anything."

"Mae will not like that. She does not like me," Kente said removing her hands from her face.

"Mae will not harm you. I own her and she will do as I say," he said sharply to her.

"Then I will do as you say because you *own* me."

James looked down at Kente and pulled her up to him.

"No why did you say that? I meant it another way. And yes, I own you on paper, but in my heart, you belong to no one. But tonight, I made you my wife and we will be together." He kissed her.

"I will never use those words around you again."

Chapter 12

Abenaa

Abenaa woke up earlier than Kodia and decided to go for walk in the woods. She needed to talk to nature, to ground herself to mother earth. The owners of the resort had opened a path with markers so that their guests would be able to walk and venture out a nature walk around the lake. They had done all that they could do to preserve the trees and keep them intact without clearing so much of the greenery.

Abenaa had been ecstatic when she had found this place. Her mother had left instructions on where she had to take Kodia before she had died. In her mind she knew that she had to free herself from jealousy, but her heart was speaking to her about her own power.

She had been the one who had went through several initiations to gain the knowledge and of the spirits. Not Kodia! She had been the one to kill the ego and to allow herself to *be activated.* Not Kodia! The blood of *Kente* flowed in her veins just as her sister, but Kodia did not want this. She did not want to be fully involved.

Before her mother had died, of unknown causes, she trusted her oldest daughter to do what was right by her sister. To protect her in spiritual matters and to help her come into her full power. Yes, Kodia looked just like *Kente*, but *Kente* had not been awakened inside of her.

Reincarnation was funny that way. A person could be reborn back into an animal or another body with no memory of who they were in the past. That soul would have to be *activated* in order to remember. Some say that it starts from where the soul left off, while others believe that they are just simply trying to get right repeatedly.

I do not have any idea why *Kente* would want to come back? She had been given the power at sixteen to transcend into a powerful goddess. But what did she forget? What mission did she not complete?

Well it really did not matter anymore. This was a new time a new era, and there was no need to do as the elders had done. Kodia was twenty-seven not sixteen. Who know if the rite would even work anyway?

Abenaa kept walking on her path deep in her thoughts. She walked closer to the lake and as she approached the water's edge, she moved closer. Taking off her shoes she stepped into the water allowing the coolness of the water to refresh her. Abenaa closed her eyes and when she opened them, she saw a woman floating on the water dressed like an old slave. She blinked her eyes, for she was never able to see spirits, and now she was seeing this woman floating on the water. She blinked her eyes again to make sure that she was seeing correctly. The woman was still there floating. The woman moved closer to her. Abenaa took two steps back as the woman had moved directly in her front of her.

"What do you want?" Abenaa asked with fear in her voice.

"In due time l will tell ya'. Just open up and let me in," the woman said.

Before Abenaa could protest she felt a sharp pain in the back of her neck, then it moved across her forehead. She tried to raise her hand to her head, but it felt like something was holding her arms. The pain lasted for a minute, then Abenaa was released. The floating woman had disappeared.

She glanced around at the lake as she watched three hawks fly over the water towards her. The hawks were extremely big and at first, she felt a little frightened as they kept flying in her direction. She remembered that she was a high priestess, and she should have no fear. She walked over to a tree and sat down beside it.

The three hawks landed at her feet and transformed into the three sisters from yesterday. They were shape shifters.

"You almost ruined our plans!" Abenaa said to them.

"We had no idea that she was the splitting image of the goddess," one of the sisters answered. Her name was Sania.

"You did not describe her likeness to us," one of the other sisters answered. Her name was Ebony.

"We reacted the way we were taught to react when she returned to us," the last sister said. Her name was Crystal.

"Well you all scared her shitless," Abenaa replied.

"Are we still assisting you in the ritual Saturday night?" Ebony asked.

Abenaa looked at her agitated. "Yes, I need your help. Nothing has changed."

"One more thing sister," Sania said.

"Yes?" Abenaa said.

"We saw a likeness of *Kente's* mate staring at us after you two left," Sania answered.

"A likeness? What do you mean?" Abenaa asked her.

"He looked just like *James* and he was staring at Kodia as if he wanted to pursue her," Crystal answered.

"He must be a reincarnation of *James*, because they looked identical!" Ebony exclaimed.

"Did he follow us?" Abenaa said getting up from the ground.

"Yes," Sania answered.

"Thank you for letting me know. This really changes things now. Everything happens for a reason and he is here for her. I will speak to you all on Saturday night," Abenaa said dismissing them. The sisters transformed back into hawks and flew away.

So those were his footprints that she had seen leading into the woods. If what they say is true, then him being here is not a coincidence. The spirits are more powerful than she could ever imagined, and this man is meant to be here.

Abenaa began walking back to the path. She needed to complete this walk and speak to her guides. It appeared as if the spirits were not going to answer the questions that had previously popped in her mind.

Chapter 13

Mae

James's father had not bought Mae from an auction block. Mae had been given to his father when she was a little girl. His father had brought her home one night and kept her in the house with him. Mae had been only twelve years old when James had been born.

The *big momma* of the house had taken Mae in and had begun teaching her how to work juju. She began showing her and teaching her about what herbs were poisonous like mandrake and what herbs could make you invisible to the Master.

Big Momma had a white father and she made sure that everyone knew it. James's father stayed in her bed more than his wife. Big Momma made sure that everyone knew that as well. Big Momma hated his wife and she wanted to be able to sleep in the big bed.

The night of the delivery of James, Mae hated the fact that she had been given the task of poisoning the *master's* wife during her delivery. She had slipped the poisonous herb in her tea to try to calm her nerves. Big Momma had instructed her to get her to drink the tea to help her with labor pains. A few minutes after the birth, she had closed her eyes and died. She never got the opportunity to cradle her baby boy.

Big Momma had conceived from *the master* and was so excited. She did not want any other slave woman to carry his child, so she placed some powerful juju on the others to stop them from conceiving from *the master*. This she also taught to Mae.

But Big Momma had the grave mistake of teaching Mae the uses of the poisonous herbs. Mae had used the poison on Big Momma, and she died the same way *the master's* wife had died. But the baby that Big Momma was carrying died as well. Mae had given the child to the spirits as a blood sacrifice to have all Big Momma's power transferred to her. Not only her power, but she also took her place in the master's bed.

When James became of age, Mae would sneak into his room and climb in bed with him too. She was much older than him and she seduced him. Mae had been James's first and as she got older, she began to get jealous of him sleeping with the other slave women on the plantation.

The spirits had told her that she would not be able to conceive because of her wicked deeds, so she conjured the juju spell to have any woman who laid with James to not be able to give him a child. Over the last five years no woman gave James a child. James had figured this out and he stopped sleeping with Mae.

Now he had brought Kente into the house and had her living in there as if she was his white wife. She hated that young evil witch. Kente had carried out something that she had never did, she had contained *Marinette* in her body. How dare she?

Kente had begun helping others with her juju and this was especially threatening to Mae. Kente's juju was more powerful that hers and this really made her angry. She still had a few that was on her side on plantation, but she wanted them all to come back to her.

Mae was more jealous of the girl now because of John's love for her. Tomorrow night they would be doing a drum ceremony for

Marinette and that would be the night that she would get rid of Kente.

Mae knew that the other plantation owners frowned on white men taking black wives, so she sent a note by one of the workers to the neighboring plantation to let the white men know that John had taken a black slave wife. She knew they would come and remove Kente from the plantation and take her away from John. Her plan was in motion.

Chapter 14

Kente

Kente loved being in that big white house with James. Even though she was a young, he treated her with so much tender love and respect. Mae was being her usual self by side glancing her and being rude and disrespectful. Several times James had to correct her on her attitude towards Kente. All the other workers of the house loved her, and she would do small juju spells to help them.

Kente had no idea on what she was doing but *Marinette* would take over and teach her. They had begun coming to her more and only a few were still going to see Mae. She was not trying to steal her people from her, but they all hated her arrogance.

Kente was about to turn sixteen in two days, and she was so excited. Mae had told her that she was planning the drumming ceremony to be at the rock that she had laid upon and that they would also celebrate her birthday.

At *her* home, her mother would have a huge celebration for her. People from the neighboring villages would have come from miles around to celebrate her momentous day. There would be beaded necklaces placed around her neck, with sacred dances made in her honor to the ancestors. This would also be the night that she would be able to choose her mate for life and they both would sit on the great stools together. Kente had no idea how it was going to be here in this land.

Kente was sitting in the parlor when Jacob entered smiling.

"How ya' doing missus?" he asked her.

"I am ok Jacob," she answered, smiling at him. "Still trying to get use to this place."

"Well you are fitting in quite nicely," he replied.

"I know, but I am very excited about my birthday," she paused. "I wish I was home with my Nana and Baba. My birthday would be so grand."

Jacob walked over to her and sat down beside her. He took her hand into his. Kente had become to him like a daughter in the brief time that she had been there. He felt this need to protect her and he wanted to keep Mae from her.

"Master James has something planned really nice for you. I know that it may not be like home, but it will be really nice."

Kente looked down at his hands enveloping hers.

"Jacob thank you for all the kindness you have shown me since my arrival."

"I know how it is to be taken from one place and brought to another. I have not always been here myself."

She looked at him quizzically. "Please tell me where you are from?"

"I come from Nigeria. I am Igbo. My name is Akannam Malenke son of Obi Akache Malenke," he said to her proudly.

Kente bowed her head giving honor to his name.

"But they call me Jacob," he said smiling.

This cause a grin to spread across her face as well. He could be quite humorous at times.

"I feel like I am meeting you for the first time," she said to him.

Jacob smiled. Taking her hand, he kissed it gently.

"So, what do we have here?" Mae asked walking into the parlor.

Jacob released her hand and stood up. "Just a quick visit."

Mae walked over to the window and moving the curtain back, she looked out the window. "Glad it was me and not Master James."

Jacob looked back at me and walked out the parlor without saying goodbye.

Kente stood up and moved towards Mae. She stopped looking out the window and turned around to face her.

"Why do you hate me so?" Kente asked her.

"I do not like the way you look. You are evil. I know that you did something to James to get him to love you," she said sneering at her.

"I cannot help the fact that I was born this way. I cannot help the fact that *James* cares for me like that."

Mae began walking towards her. "I hate that you carry *Marinette* inside you, and you stole my people from me!"

Kente began backing away from her, but then she felt *Marinette* stirring inside of her and she stood my ground.

"You sound like just like these white men when you said that. They are our people! You have just as much power as I do but you do not know how to direct that energy in a more helpful way. I apologize for your hate." Kente turned around and walked out the parlor leaving her standing there with her mouth wide open. She prayed that *Marinette* will protect from her wrath.

Chapter 15

Kodia

I woke up feeling refreshed and not as tired as I was on yesterday. I slipped out of bed and went to see if Abenaa was up.

"Abenaa," I said loudly calling out her name.

There was no answer. I walked into her room and she was not there. She must have went jogging or took a morning walk. She loves speaking to her spirits during the rise of the morning sun.

I could smell fresh coffee and I went into the kitchen to pour me a cup. I walked back to the living room and went outside on the porch. I sat down in the rocking chair. I closed my eyes and inhaled the fresh morning air. I could feel it surging through my body and enhancing my lungs.

When I opened my eyes there was a man standing on the stairs. The sun was blocking his face. I stood up and walked towards him. He moved closer as well and I could see his face. It was the man from my dreams.

"C-can I help you?" I asked him, stuttering on my words.

He smiled at me and I did not smile back.

"Hi, my name is William, but you can call me Will," he said to me.

"You did not answer my question. How can I help you?"

William smiled again. He already loved her abruptness. She was a woman after his own heart.

"I do not need your help. I saw you in Asheville and I got on some stalker shit and followed you here. My hotel is not far from here."

"Hmm that do sound like some *stalker shit*," I said to him.

I must have struck a nerve with him because I could feel him becoming nervous.

"Is there something you wanted to chat with me about?" I asked him.

"No and yes," he answered. "I just want to know do you date white guys and if so, would you be willing to go out on a date with me?"

I always dated black men and never would dare stepping

outside of my race. Especially knowing that if it was not for the white man, my people would not have ended up in this country being slaves. Besides I was dark as hell and what would a white man want with me but sex.

"No, I have never been out with a white man, but I would love to go out on a date with you." Where did that come from? I was not going to say that, but it was if I could not control my tongue.

"Great," he said happily. "I will be here to pick you up around 7."

"Pick who up?" Abenaa asked walking up on the porch.

"Will this be my sister Abenaa. Abenaa this is Will," I said introducing them.

Will stuck his hand out waiting on a handshake, but Abenaa twirled her hand instead.

"I do not shake hands with people, but I do acknowledge your presence," Abenaa said to him.

"Oh ok," Will said placing his hand in his pocket.

"Will is staying at a hotel around here and he asked me to

go out with him later. I told him that I would," I said to her.

Abenaa looked Will up and down. This must have been the man that the sisters were talking about. He did indeed favor her ancestor *James*. He was tall about six foot five, and he had a long beard with green eyes.

"Well we did come up here to have fun, so why the hell not!" Abenaa exclaimed.

"Damn she sounded happy," I thought to myself.

"Well great," Will replied. "I will see you around seven o'clock."

Will walked down the stairs and got into his truck. He was so happy that this beautiful woman was going to be his for the night.

Abenaa turned around and walked into the cottage. I followed her. She went into the kitchen and got her a bottle of water.

"I am glad that you did not act all stuck up ," she said to me drinking from the bottle of water.

"I wanted to say no, because I love my brothers, but I

couldn't."

"You need to go out and have fun," she said to me.

"Well we are in Asheville and who will know that I went out with a white guy," I said to her.

"Me," she replied laughing.

"What happens in Asheville, stays in Asheville," I said laughing back at her.

"Yep. What happens here *stays* here," my sister said.

I felt like they're was a double meaning behind her words. I walked back outside and sat on the porch.

Chapter 16

James

Tonight, was a special night for Kente. Mae had told me everything she needed for her birthday celebration and I made sure that she had everything she asked. James could not believe how nice Mae had been about celebrating her birthday.

Mae was the first woman that James had sex with, and he would always care for her, but he was deeply in love with Kente. When she gave herself to him willing, James could not resist her. James needed her, no craved to be inside of her every minute of the day. Her body melted into his and he knew that he would love her forever.

There was going to be drumming and dancing. James would get to watch Kente dance and enjoy herself with her people. James also knew that if the other slave owners knew that he had taken up with a black slave that they would probably jail him. But he did not care. He needed Kente in his life and that was all that matter.

His father had left him land up in the North Carolina

mountains near Asheville, and if there was trouble, he would take

Kente there and live with her in peace. He would probably take some

of the slaves if they wanted to follow them. They had been very

loyal to him and his family and he only wanted them to have a goof

life outside of slavery.

Chapter 17

Mae

Everything was going as *she* had planned. The other plantations had received information about James's love for a slave girl. Once and for all she would be renewed by the removal of Kente and the people would be hers to control again.

She walked outside and moved to the edge of the porch leaning against the rail. She glanced around as the other slaves' hustle and bustle about preparing the festivities tonight for Kente's birthday. They were all such idiots to her being so mild and meek and humble to the white man's doctrine, the *Holy Bible.*

Ever since she arrived here, all the Master ever gave her to read was that book. All that book did was teach her people how to be better slaves. That book kept them in slavery in bondage and it would keep destroying her people for centuries to come. She cared but she did not care. All she wanted was the power and respect to control everyone and make the best of their situation.

Mae walked over to the white rocking chair and sat down.

She closed her eyes and slowly began to rock.

Chapter 18

Kente

Kente was looking out the window watching Mae rock in the chair. She could sense that Mae had not change and she could sense that something was coming. Even though the sun was shining brightly and today was perfect, she had this feeling of a strong sense of earnest to communicate with the spirit that was inside of her.

Kente turned around and began walking up the stairs. She knew that it was *Marinette* pulling her for she must have wanted to speak to her as well. She went into the room and pulled all the curtains drawing the room darker. *Marinette* loved the darkness for it was soothing to her eyes. Unlike Mae, she did not need to draw symbols with white flour to invoke her. She walked over to the dresser bureau and grabbed the small silver handheld mirror in her hands. Walking to the middle of the floor she sat down and peered into the mirror. She closed her eyes then opened them; *Marinette* was staring back at her.

Kente did not know that *Marinette* was going to be this

beautiful as she stared at her. Her hair was long and bushy but tamed. Her complexion was dark, but her eyes danced with fiery flames.

"What is this that I am feeling?" Kente asked *Marinette*.

"There is going to be trouble tonight during the party," she spoke to her.

"I knew I was sensing something!" Kente exclaimed.

"Yes, but you and a few others will be ok," Marinette said.

"What about James?" Kente asked.

"I need for you to look in the floorboard under your bed. There is a brown bottle filled with water from the footprint of a wolf. You will give this to James to drink," Marinette instructed.

"What will this to do to him?" she asked the Loa.

" When he drinks this , he will be able to protect us. Mae had collected this water to be able to have shape shifters to control. This will cause James to shape shift into a wolf and he will protect you. Werewolves are my guardians."

"I am aware of shape shifters living in my land. There is a

tribe which can turn into hyenas. Did not think that it existed here on this land as well," Kente replied.

"Some stories are true some are not, but trust me this one is," Marinette said. *"Now get ready for they are coming to get you. Do not be afraid for I am with you child, and this will be over soon."* *Marinette vanished.*

Kente heard a knock at the door and walked over to answer it. It was two house girls coming to help her get dressed for the ritual. One of the girls was carrying a box and she walked over to the bed and laid it down. Kente walked over to the bed and opened the box. She pulled out a white dress and white cloth. The other house girl came over and told her to put the dress on. Kente began removing her clothes as they began to help her get dress. They then took the white cloth and wrapped her hair up with it. Kente walked over to the mirror ad looked at herself. It was amazing how white made you look so pure. The house girls opened the door, gesturing to Kente that it was time to leave. Kente glanced in the mirror one more time seeing the fire in your eyes and she knew that all was going to be okay.

Chapter 19

James

James stood at the bottom of the stairs watching Kente as she began to descend towards him. She was more beautiful then he could ever imagine. He was more captivated by her beauty then the first day that he had seen her. He loved this young girl no young woman with all his heart and he could not wait until the ritual was over to have her in his bed.

Kente got down to the last step and James embraced her. She hugged him back and then whispered in his ear. "Take this bottle and drink from it. I do not know how tonight will go, but this will protect you if anything evil happens tonight."

James took the bottle from her hands and drunk it down. He then placed the bottle inside his right pocket. He trusted Kente with all his heart. He began to fill a tight squeeze on his heart as it felt like someone was gripping it tight. He grabbed his chest as if he was having a heart attack. Kente grabbed his arm and placed her hand on his chest. A worried look came across her eyes as she became a little afraid of his plight. Just as the pain hit him, it left him, and he gathered his composure once again.

"I am alright," he said assuring her.

Kente nodded at him as he extended his hand out and commenced to escort her to ritual. James began to feel this strong power take him over and it was as if his strength had magnified in his body. No matter what happened tonight, he was going to protect her no matter what the cost.

Chapter 20

Mae

Mae stood up from the rocking chair which she was sitting in and began walking to down the path. When she came to the clearing in the woods, she moved to the middle of the circle. She walked close to the fire that Jacob had started and watched with envy and hate as James escorted Kente towards her. The two-house girls that were walking behind them, both separated and went to join the others alongside the circle.

Mae instructed James to move back to the side for only she and Kente could stand in the circle. James kissed Kente on the hand then did as he was instructed. Mae looked over at Jacob and told him to bring over the two wooden crates that were waiting beside the drummers. Jacob brought them over and sat them down on the ground beside Mae. He reached into his trouser pocket and pulled out a long silver bladed knife. He handed it to Mae and he too fell back into his place with the drummers.

The drummers began slowly beating on the drums as Mae

took a brown bottle of liquor and poured it near the veve drawn with white cornmeal on the ground. She then took a swig of the liquor and sprayed Kente with it from her mouth.

"This is for all the people's blood that was spilt on this land."

Kente begin to feel a small breeze embracing her body.

Mae opened the first crate and she pulled out a huge rooster. She began moving back and forth with the bird facing east. She looked up in the sky at the full moon.

"By the power of the Miss Moon, Fair Venus and the Brilliant Sun I call you. By the power of Miss Magie who proceeds Loso-Meji, in the name of Negress Loko, Negress Gba-a-Dou, Negress Yalode, Lihsah, Negress Rainbow, La Siren, La Baleine; Mother Erzulie, Negress Freda, and Maitress Marinette I call you all," Mae chanted. She then broke the neck of the rooster, its feet and wings. She then rubbed the bird on the veve, then she brings the bird to her mouth and tears off its head. As blood squirts all over her clothes and face. She then throws it on the ground.

Mae moves to the other crate and pulls out a black snake.

Jacob begins to beat on the drums harder in a fierce rhythm as Mae starts to dance around Kente holding the snake over her head. Mae began to feel the power of the spirits moving inside of her, but they were not the ones that she wanted.

Kente could feel *Marinette* rising inside of her as she tossed her head back and her eyes began to roll in the back of her head. Mae felt *Marinette* and she began to chant louder and dancing more wildly as Kente began to levitate a few inches off the ground. The two-house girls joined the dance as they stripped themselves of the clothes and began dancing as if they had been possessed with the loas as well.

Mae stopped dancing when she saw the five white men standing in the woods watching. She needed to sacrifice the snake for her to obtain *Marinette* inside of her. She needed to transfer the head to herself. She moved closer to Kente.

Marinette had completely taken over Kente and she laughed in her face. *"Do you really think that by sacrificing that snake that you can take me form her? You're a stupid fool!"* Marinette *snatched the snake from her.*

Mae fell back as *Marinette* watched the fear explode in her eyes.

James rushed to Kente's side and as he did, he saw the other plantation owners emerge from the woods. This startled him for he had no idea why they were here.

"So, it true that you been taking up with this nigga bitch and forgetting that you are her *master!*" one of the white men said. He motioned to one of the men to take James.

The man approached James, but he was too fast and punched him in the face. The man fell backwards as the other two attempted to grab him and place a noose around his neck. James saw the man who had spoken to him reach out and try to grab Kente.

"Come here you witch nigga!" he said angrily.

James jumped towards them feeling the power of his strength taking him over, and as he did the bottle fell out of his pocket. Mae saw the bottle and screamed. "NO!"

James began to feel his body changing as his arms became

hairy and his jaws became unhinged as sharp teeth began to protrude from his mouth. He fell to the ground in pain as he could feel his body shifting into an animal. He turned his head up looking at the moon.

Everyone watched in fright as they saw James transformed into the beast. Everyone except Kente for she was still empowered by *Marinette*. James stood up and howled at the moon. The white men tried to run, but James grabbed them all and snatched out their hearts.

Mae ran towards James with the silver blade, knowing that silver would kill him. As she raised the blade in the air, James turned on her and with one bite ripping out her throat. Mae fell to the ground holding her throat. Upon seeing this, the slaves began to run in fear of their lives. They had never seen anything like this, and they were scared. James ran to Kente and picked her up. He carried her off into the woods.

Chapter 21

Kente

Kente slowly opened her eyes as the sun began to rise and shine through the leaves. She was laying on the ground beside a tall tree and she felt achy but well. She sat up and James was lying beside her. She looked down at herself and notice that she was covered in blood. What had happened last night? She had no recollection of what had taken place.

James began to stir as he woke up and grabbed Kente close to him. His grasp was strong and he eased up after seeing Kente flinch.

"Sorry, are you okay?" he asked her.

"Yes," she answered. "What happened and why are we here?" she asked him.

"Last night during the ritual, the other plantations owners showed up. It was only five of them."

"No, we got to flee, they will hang you and me!" she exclaimed. Kente arose from the ground.

"Kente I killed them all," James said in anguish. "They tried to take me, but I changed into this beast, into this wolf and I overtook them. Mae tried to kill me, but I ripped out her throat. I was this beast, but I had my senses. All I wanted to do was to protect you, but I murdered people in the process."

Kente looked at James as tears fell from his eyes. "It's my fault for the liquid that you drunk from that bottle was water from a wolfs print and it was meant to transform you."

"So, you knew this was going to happen to me?" he asked in shock.

"Yes," she answered in shame. *"Marinette* told me to give it to you to protect us. She knew that danger was coming for us and that we needed to be protected from our enemies."

James stood up on his feet and took her hands inside of his. "I could never be angry with you my love. It was painful for me to turn, but it worked. I was able to kill everyone who sought after us."

"What do we do now?" she asked him. "Everyone on the planation saw what happened last night. They are afraid. What we going to do?"

"I have land up in the North Carolina mountains close to Tennessee. We can take all that we need and live there. I will ask those who are not afraid to come with us, but as free people and not my slaves."

"Do you think that they will want to go?" she asked him.

"Yes, perhaps not all of them, but most of them. We will start our own town where those who want to love whomever they want can love."

Kente wrapped her arms around James hugging him tight. She closed her eyes as she heard *Marinette* whisper to her, " *This is what I come for the freedom of our people, and all will worship us.* "

Chapter 22

Kodia

I sat on the porch waiting for my *date* to show up. I was excited but nervous at the same time. This was going to be my first time going out with a white man and I was concerned about what the brothers would say when they saw us together. I had poured me a glass of Merlot and was sipping on it when Abenaa walked out on the porch.

"Your nervous sis ?" she asked me.

"Hell yeah," I answered. "This is so different for me, but yet I feel like I should be going out with him."

"What do you mean?"

"I feel like I know him. Like maybe he has been waiting for me all my life. I cannot explain it, but only time will tell if we were meant to be. I just got to get over this race complex and then I know that it will be all good."

Abenaa walked over to me and placed her arm around my shoulder. "I think, no believe that the universe has a way of allowing us to see that sometimes the unusual is exactly what we need in our lives. Just go with the flow and all will be irie."

We both looked up at the same time as we saw William pulled up in his truck. He stepped out the truck looking more gorgeous than when I first had laid eyes on him. He was wearing black cargo shorts with a nice button-down shirt. It also looked like he had gotten a haircut.

"Speak of the devil," my sister said under her breath as he got out of the truck and walked towards her.

I smiled a little but was curious as to why she would refer to him as the devil when she hardly knew him. I walked down from the porch meeting him halfway and he embraced me giving me the biggest and warmest embrace I had ever felt from a man.

"You must be really happy to see me," I said giggling.

"Damn right I am. I been waiting for this evening all day. I just want to make sure that you have a real good time. You will not have to worry about anything."

"So, Will, what time do you plan on having my sister back?"

Abenaa asked him.

Before he could answer I spoke. "I am a grown woman and I will be back when I get back," I answered for him smiling.

Abenaa laughed. "I know that sis, I was just being protective. We really do not know much about him."

"I promise you, that I will protect her with my own life. I could never harm her in any way. But I will have her back before 3 a.m. I promise," Will said.

"Damn what you got planned?" I said, with curiosity in my voice.

"I have three sisters and they all taught me how to be a perfect gentleman. Do not worry you will have fun with me."

Will took me by the hand and guided me to his truck. He opened the door for me and helped me get in the truck.

"A gentle man," I said to him.

Will walked around to the driver's side and climbed in. "As long as you are riding with me, I will *always* open the door for you."

As we drove down the road leading to the highway will took

my hand in his, and he held my hand all the way to Asheville.

Chapter 23

Abenaa

Abenaa watched them as they drove away. She walked backed inside the house and sat down the sofa. This was just a little too much for her right now. Will looked exactly like *James*, and he was already acting like he was head over heels in love with Kodia. She could tell that it would be impossible for her to get rid of him.

She laid her head back against the pillow and closed her eyes. Suddenly there was a loud knock as if someone was knocking at the front door. Abenaa arose from the sofa and walked to answer the door. "Who is it?" she asked standing behind the door.

No answer.

She walked back to the sofa and then she heard 3 knock this time. Abenaa walked to the door and snatched it open but there was no one standing there. She peeked her head around the door but saw no one. She closed the door and turned around towards the sofa.

Abenaa begin to feel the hair rise on the back of her neck as she felt a small breeze blow past her and move in the direction of her bedroom. At that moment Abenaa wished she had not opened the door. Ever since she had come from her walk at the lake, she had been feeling off. If she had been in her right mind, she would have never opened the door for that spirit that had just walked into the cottage.

Suddenly it felt like someone had yanked on her arm and it was pulling her towards her bedroom. Abenaa tried to fight against the force, but it kept pulling her. When she was standing in front of the mirror on the dresser, it let her go.

Abenaa placed her hands on the dresser using it as a prop to gain her composure. She had never felt this type of energy before and it really had scared the shit out of her. The energy felt like what she had encountered at the lake. The spirits had always communicated with her in a calm way, but this was something else.

Suddenly she heard a woman's voice speak to her. "Abenaa."

She raised her eyes up and looked at the mirror staring at her reflection. She began to fee a tightness around her throat, and she grasped at her throat as it felt like something was squeezing her. As she tried to grasp for air, her reflection in the mirror began to change. It was as if her eyes had become distorted. and she was in total darkness. She blinked her eyes trying to regain focus. And that is when she was what was in the mirror. It appeared to be a woman dressed in old slavery clothes. It looked like the lady whom she had seen floating on the water at the lake. The tightness around her throat began to loosen. Abenaa began to catch her breath again.

"That's right chile, relax," the woman from the mirror said.

"Wh-who are you?" Abenaa asked stammering over her words.

"I be Mae."

"Mae? Are you my Ancestor?" Abenaa asked her.

"No, but I am here to stop your sister from taking that initiation."

"Why?"

"I knew *Kente* and I hated her. She took *James* and my people from me, and I am going to make sure that she does not come back thru that gal."

Abenaa stared at Mae. "They will not allow that to happen. My *Ancestors* are powerful, and they protect us."

Mae began to chuckle. "You would do anything to contain that power that she about to get. You know it's true. I can see your deepest desire."

How did Mae know what her secret desires were? Yes, she was very jealous of Kodia and she did wish that the power was coming to her.

"See you thinking about it," Mae said to her hungrily. "I can help you get what you want and more."

Abenaa wanted that power, but she did not want to hurt her

sister. For although she coveted her power, she still loved her very much. " No, I will not allow you to hurt my sister."

"Gal you have no choice. I done already claimed your body. I was not giving you a choice!"

Abenaa tried to resist, but she felt herself losing control of her body. She began to feel the headache she felt at the lake and then she felt her consciousness being pushed to the back of her mind. She could not fight Mae from taking over her body. She fell on the floor and laid there whimpering as Mae consumed her being.

Chapter 24

Mae

Mae arose from the floor and walked over to the dresser. She began smoothing out her clothes as she adjusted herself in Abenaa's body. She smiled at herself as she began running her fingers through her hair. She could still feel Abenaa trying to fight her possession of her.

"Just let yourself sink down into that black hole and wait till I am done. Once I am done you can come back. If you had just let me take you over, I would share this body with you, but you had to resist me." Mae gazed the mirror and smiled at her image. "Well I do not know child. Maybe I will stay in here forever".

Mae heard a knock at the door, and she went to answer it.

Opening the door, she saw three women standing there with boxes in their hands.

" We bought all the stuff to perform the ritual," Sania said walking past Mae.

The other two followed their sister into the cottage. Mae stared at them as they placed the boxes on the floor and began moving the furniture to clear out space in the middle of the room.

"What's the matter with you Abenaa?" Ebony asked her. "The ritual is still on, right?"

Mae smiled at her. "I'm ok and yes we are still doing this."

"Well you are just standing there looking very puzzled," Ebony replied.

Mae walked over to Ebony and touched her face. She could feel that she had been empowered with the spirits as well as the other two women. "I got this child," she said to her.

Crystal was looking at Abenaa very strangely. She was beginning to pick up the energy of another presence in the room.

Mae turned around and saw Crystal staring at her oddly.

"Why are you looking at me like that?" she asked her.

"I just feel a different energy in here and I was just wondering where it was coming from," she answered her.

"Of course, you gonna feel a different energy in here. I just finished speaking to the Ancestors." Mae took her hands and rubbed them down her face.

"That's probably what I am feeling then," Crystal said as she stared back moving furniture.

"I feel something too, but like Abenaa said it's probably the Ancestors lingering around," Ebony said.

Mae walked over the sofa and sat down. She watched as the sisters had cleared everything out the room. They placed a small table against the wall in which they covered it with a white cloth. They filled three large goblets with water, and they placed a silver chalice in the middle of the table. Beside the chalice, Ebony place a large blade with a bone handle. Crystal began adding fruits and small cakes to the table for food for the spirits.

Mae watched in amusement as they placed candles all over

the room and one large black candle on the altar in which they had created. They did have some power but neither one of them really knew how to use the gifts which was given to them.

Sania reached into her bag and pulled out the statuette of *Kente* and placed it on the altar. Beside *Kente's* statuette she places another one of a woman dressed in a red cloak, but her face was all skeletal. This was the image of *Marinette*.

"Well I be damn," Mae thought to herself. " They have formed the likeness of *Marinette* into this thing sitting on the table. That be a sin from the good book."

Mae arose from the sofa and went an picked up the statuette of *Kente.*

"Doesn't your sister look just like her?" Sania asked her.

Mae stared at the statuette as anger began to envelop her and raising the statuette above her head, she threw it against the wall smashing it into pieces.

"What the fuck you do that for!" Sania screamed at her as she rushed to floor trying to gather up the broken parts.

Mae turned around and faced Sania. Sania had her back turned, for she was kneeling on the floor picking up the remains from the broken statuette. She picked up the bone handle blade from the table and walking over the Sania she grabbed her by hair. Sania let out a scream, as Mae pulled her head back and slit her throat. "Now we have a blood sacrifice."

Ebony and Crystal stood there is disbelief as they watched their sister's blood flow from her throat and unto the floor. Some of Sania's blood had splattered onto the white tablecloth.

"You stupid bitch!" Ebony yelled as she ran towards Mae.

Mae stood there with a wicked grin on her face as she met Ebony and plunged the blade deep into her chest. As the blade touched Ebony's heart, she gave it a twist stopping her heart from beating and Ebony fell to the floor. Crystal was standing there with her eyes close trying to shape shift. Her powers were not that strong without her two sisters.

Mae cast her eyes at Crystal and with a wave of her hand, she turned her neck completely around and Crystal dropped to the floor.

"I would have given you the blade, but I have all the blood I need."

Mae took the chalice off the table and filled it with Sania's and Ebony blood. She took three sips from it and then placed in back onto the altar. She could feel the warmness of the blood coursing through her veins, and she tilted her head back taking in their power.

Mae with her increased power, moved the ladies out the house to the backyard. She placed their bodies beside each other and began chanting over them. "I call upon you great mama to accept these offerings from me." She saw a gallon of kerosene sitting beside the house and she walked over and picked it up. Bringing it back to the witches she had just murdered; she pours kerosene over their bodies. She raises her hands over the bodies then she spit on them. The ashe from her saliva landed on them and she offered their bodies up to *Marinette*, as they were received in a fiery blaze.

Chapter 25

Kodia and William

When William pulled up in the front of the Hyatt hotel, I looked at him. "Really?"

He smiled at me. "It's not what you think beautiful," he said. He found a parking space close to the entrance and parked his truck. I sat there waiting for him to open the door. I watched as he walked around the front of the truck and opened the door for me. He held out his hand as I placed my hand in his, as he helped me from the truck.

"I really hope that you have something else planned, for I am not ready to take this step with you. Not right now", I said to him.

"Listen, I really need you to trust me because I would never do anything nor make you do anything that you are not ready for."

Something inside of me was telling me to believe in him and trust him, for he would never hurt me. But the reading from my sister was still resting in the back on my mind. "Okay," I said back to him. Taking my hand inside of his, we walked into the Hyatt.

To my surprise he had made dinner reservations at *Montford Rooftop Bar* which was located on the top floor of the hotel. This place was so gorgeous to me. I had never been to a restaurant like . Most of the men whom I had dated, had never taken me to a restaurant to eat where they had made reservations. He was really making me feel very special.

The hostess led us to our table, which was next to a huge window. This gave us a gorgeous view of the Blue Ridge Mountains and it was breathtaking. We had a great view of the sunset and I was taken back from its beauty. At that moment I felt like I had just been touched by a higher power and water began to form in my eyes.

"Are you ok beautiful?" he asked me, taking his seat across from me.

"Yes. This is just so breath taking," I answered him. I patted the corner of my eyes as I felt the tears coming forth.

"I wanted nothing but the best for you for our first date."

"I was not expecting all of this. I thought we were just going to go to *Apple Bee's* and get dinner for the price of two," I said smiling.

"Beautiful, I like that place, but I wanted to take you somewhere you had never been before. I wanted to give you a good memory."

I cast my eyes down at the menus and picked mines up. Scanning over the cocktail list, I ordered the *Summertime Magic* which had cocoa nib infused with dark rum. William ordered *Recipe for a Ghost*. It was infused with apricot. Once the server brought us our drinks, we both agreed that the cocktails were delicious.

When it was time to order our food, I decided to try the small plate and order the *smoked trout dip*. We both agreed to share the *tomato mozzarella flat bread*. The food tasted so good! William told me that the reason why he chose this restaurant for us to eat, was that they used all local ingredients in their food. For dessert, we both also shared the chocolate *toffee skillet cookie for two*.

After dinner we decided to walk around the city. The festival was still going, and I told him that I really wanted to avoid all the crowds. I especially did not want to run into those sisters from the other day. I was walking on the sidewalk on the outside nearest to the streets, and he moved me to the inside of him and took my hand.

"As long as you are walking with me, I never want you walking near the street. Some stupid driver can lose control and hit you."

"Wow you really are the perfect gentleman."

"Beautiful I do not do this for everyone. But I feel like I must protect you and keep you safe. From the first time I seen you, I wanted to get to know you and nothing was going to stop me from meeting you."

"So, are you always the type of man who gets what he wants?"

"Pretty much," William answered. "All I want right now is to enjoy where we are at this moment."

I squeezed his hand tighter and I felt a tingle down below. The way he was talking to me was turning me on, and I felt safe with him. "William, I know that this is our first date, but I really do feel like this, us, we are supposed to be like this." I stopped walking and leaned against the building. William moved closer to me and looked down at me. He was standing so close to me that I could feel his breath against my face.

"I do not know what is going on, but this feels like déjà vu. I can not explain it, but it feels like we have been here before."

I looked up at him. "Yes, it does feel like that. Its like I feel like I need to have you in my life and that maybe our souls connected in the past."

"Do you believe in past lives?" he asked me.

"Yes, I do. I have a gift for feeling and sometimes I am shown visions. But you and me, we on a different level of connection. I know that we are different with our race, but when we were at the restaurant, I saw no color."

"The same with me beautiful," William said to me. Moving closer he kissed me. His lips felt so hot and so warm that I pulled him into me, pressing my body against his tighter, as I tasted his lips. Suddenly the door to the building that we were making out on opened, and this woman with long braids stepped out. I released

William and he stepped back.

"I been waiting for you two," she said to us.

"Waiting for us?" I asked.

"Yes, waiting for you both. My name is Wisdom, and this is my botanica. The Ancestors have a message for you both." Wisdom gestured for us to enter her shop.

"What could it hurt," William said as he escorted me into the shop.

Chapter 26

The Message

When I walked into her shop, I notice that she really did not have a lot of different goods to sell. There were different color candles lined up on a shelf against the left side of the wall. Some of the candles had different saints labeled n them. On the right side of the store she had several figurines that she was selling as well. Towards the back of the store was a shelf lined with books. Also, she had a small glass case housing several bags of herbs and magical baths.

In the corner of the shop was a small round table with a white candle burning on it. She had a straw mat with a regular deck of playing cards on it. "So, she did readings like my sister did," I thought to myself.

"Is this message for the both of us together and is these separate messages?" William asked her. He seemed to be a little frustrated for having been interrupted from our kiss.

"Come and take a seat at the table. I know that you have

questions, but my message is for the both of you," Wisdom said to us.

I looked at William and taking my hand into his we both walked to the table and took a seat. Wisdom picked up the cards and began shuffling them. She placed the deck close to our mouths and instructed us to blow on the cards. William and I both blew on the cards then she spread them across the table face down. She pulled seven cards from the spread-out deck and turned them over.

As I looked at the cards all of them were face cards. Wisdom began interpreting the meaning of the cards to us.

"The *Queen of Clubs* represent you," she said looking at me. "You are very beautiful, and you have a generous gift. You must have more confidence in your abilities and the gifts that have been given to."

"The *Jack of Hearts* represents you," she said looking at William. "You have a lot of things to accomplish in life , but you also are in love with her."

I glanced over at William and his face was turning red. "He

loves me?" I thought to myself.

"Now you see the *Queen of Hearts* and the *King of Hearts* both represents two spirits who love you and are here with you both. It is no accident that you two are together right now. I do not know if you believe in reincarnation but both of you carry great spirits who shared a great love and they are with you now"'

At that moment the flame on the candle began to raise higher and I felt chills. I glanced over at William and I could see goosebumps on his arms. I wanted to not believe what she was saying, and I tried to speak to her it felt like something was preventing me from speaking. "*Listen*", I heard a voice say to me.

"The *Ace of Spades* are telling you that there is death around you, and emotions are going to come to a head. You both are about to face a great confrontation which will almost tear you apart."

"There was the Ace of Spades again." I thought to myself.

"What do you mean death and a confrontation?" I heard William ask her. I was still unable to speak.

"Do you see how the *Queen of Spades* is next to the *Queen of*

Diamonds?" she asked him.

"Yes."

"Well even though they are two different cards, they both represent the same person. The *Queen of Diamonds* is your sister Kodia," she said looking at me now. "She has been hiding something from you. She has been very jealous of what you will receive from your Ancestor who lives inside of you." I wanted to scream and tell this bitch that she did not know what she was talking about. All I had was my sister and she would never do anything to hurt me.

Wisdom was looking at me as if she was reading my mind. "I know that the spirits have your voice but listen to me *please*," she pleaded. "The *Queen of Spades* represents this dark spirit which had attached herself to your sister. She is on some type of revenge and she wants to stop *Mama Kente* from returning."

Suddenly the hairs on the back of my neck began to rise. I remember the witches who were calling me that, and I recalled the trance I had went into. Wisdom got up from the table and walked over to the shelve where all her books were seated. She removed an old book from the shelf and brought it back to the table. Opening the book, she stopped when she came to a picture.

When she turned the book around for both of us to see the picture, I gasped. There was a woman standing beside a white man with a beard on the porch of a huge white house. They both looked exactly like William and me. It was like we were staring at ourselves in a mirror.

"Who is that?" William asked her in a calm voice.

"What you are looking at is *James* and *Mama Kente*. *Mama Kente* was a slave woman who belonged to *James*. He fell in love with her and he treated her like she was his wife. *Mae*, who was his slave as well became jealous and she tried to destroy them. *Mama Kente* was empowered by *Marinette* and *Mae* was jealous of that power. *James* and *Mama Kente* fled with other slaves up here to Asheville. With the help of some Cherokees, they were able to live their lives on the mountain around the lake."

I looked at William and he gripped my hand tighter.

"*Mama Kente* is your great ancestor, and she is waiting to

give you all her power. She was so powerful that the locals developed a church for her, and she was worshipped. The natives here began following her teachings and way of life. Mama Kente had the power to heal and move mountains. She could speak to the animals, the trees and move energy with her mind. Her patron, *Marinette,* would speak directly to her. She would appear to her as a skeleton dressed in red and black. She had control over the dead bones and brought them back to life."

Thoughts began to race through my mind. I was taken back to my dreams in which I saw the skeletal hands pulling me under. The house was exactly like the house in my dreams. "Please give me my voice back," I said to myself in my mind. The tightness began to leave my throat and I was able to speak.

"I have been dreaming about these skeletal hands coming out from under the ground and I have been dreaming about that house," I said.

"Yes, I know. The hands that were pulling you, were trying to protect you and stop you from entering that house. The dark spirit that has your sister was in there hiding waiting on you."

I stood up removing my hand from William's, I placed both my hands on the table.

"So, you trying to tell me thatt not only is my sister jealous of me, but some dark spirit is trying to kill me! I just cannot believe that," I said shaking my head.

William stood up beside me and tried to calm me down. I was becoming agitated and even though this was making sense, I could not believe that my sister was jealous of me and would hurt me. But from the *last* dream that I had, I really do believe that a *dark spirit* is after me.

"I do not believe in magic, but I do believe in what *I* feel," William said looking at me. "From the first time that I laid my eyes on you, I was drawn to you. I have never in my life felt the urge to want to be with someone as strongly as I felt the desire to be with you. I have never wanted to protect someone like I wanted to protect you. Maybe this is crazy, but I feel that we need to listen to her and let her help us."

I knew that what William was saying was true because I could feel the emotion in his voice, but it's hard to believe that my sister would hurt me.

"Please the both of you sit down," Wisdom said to us. "I am not finished with the message, but first I must explain those witches that you saw. Those witches belong to a group of people who follow the teaches of your ancestor. "

I sat back down in my chair and William followed me. "How do you know what happened to me ?"

"*They* tell me. They, meaning my spirits who serve me. I channel the dead and they are the ones telling me that you need to prepare for what's coming."

"Please tell us what's coming," William said to Wisdom. "I do not know about Kodia, but I believe you and I am going to do whatever it takes to protect her."

Wisdom turned to face William and she took his hands into hers. I could feel chills coming over my body again, and the flame from the candle began flickering again. I looked at Wisdom and her head began to arch back as I watch her eye lids began to flutter. Guttural sounds began to come from her mouth as she began to sway back and forth. I looked at William, and his face were turning red from the grip that Wisdom had on his hands. I reached towards him to snatch him away, but as I began to do so. Wisdom began to speak.

"I come to bring you no harm but to warn you. You must allow your power to come forth and you must not be afraid. Trust in William for I am with him and I will protect you," she said in a deep male voice. As I listened to whatever it was that had spoken through her, I began to see a clear smoke float from her mouth, and she released William's hands. William rubbed his hands and looked at me. I stared back at him.

"Kodia you must listen to spirit. That was *James* who spoke through me and I used William to channel him."

"I may not understand all of this, but I do know that something spiritual is taking place and happening in my life. I want to believe all that you say, but I just cannot get past the *sister trying to hurt me part.*"

"Look beautiful," William said facing me. "I believe what is going on here and I am going to listen to the message." He turned to face Wisdom. "What must I do to protect her?"

Wisdom arose from the table and walked back into a door which led into a room behind her counter in the store. When she returned, she was holding a small brown bottle with cork in it. It was filled with liquid and she handed it to William. "Please drink this and this will give you all the power you need to protect her."

"What is in that bottle?" I asked Wisdom.

"It is water, rainwater from a wolves paw print."

"Really," I said. "How is that supposed to help him protect me?"

"*James* was given a bottle like this to drink from and he was granted strength and power to protect Kente. This liquid enabled him to shape shift into a werewolf and he destroyed all the slavers who tried to kill them."

"So, you are telling me that this will turn me into a fucking werewolf!" William exclaimed. "I thought that was just make believe, some television shit like *The Originals* that my sister is always watching on Netflix. If I drink that, I will be a werewolf for life!"

"I do not want him to drink that!" I said angrily to her.

"If he does not drink this then he will be unable to stop your death," Wisdom spoke quietly to me. "*Marinette* will come and when she does, she will take over you and you need to be protected from that dark force that is wanting to destroy you."

Before I could say another word, William grabbed the bottle, removing the cork he turned the bottle to his mouth and drunk all the liquid that was inside.

"No," I cried as tears began to run down my face. But it was to late, he had finished it all. I looked at William and he grinned at me. "See beautiful still me."

"I did not want you to sacrifice your life for me. At least your human life. We just met and I now I have to get through this dark shit and you…"

"And I love you," he said finishing my sentence.

"Remember Kodia," Wisdom said to me. "Do not be afraid to use your gifts and pay attention to the energy and the feelings around you. Do not doubt but trust this man." She removed a medallion that she was wearing and placed it around my neck. "This will give you protection and help you to focus. "The medallion was shaped like a triangle and had symbols engraved onto it.

"But you never told us what this dark force is that has taken her?" I asked Wisdom.

"*Kente* and *James* had an enemy. She was there before Kente arrived and she was *James* lover once. She had powers like *Kente's*, but she was used her gifts for evil. The spirits shunned her and when she tried to call down *Marinette*, *Marinette* went to Kente. she seeks to destroy your bloodline and get the spirits back on her side. It's Mae."

"This is still all confusing to me, but I do feel that you could be telling us the truth."

"Kodia just pay attention to your dreams for your dreams are messages from the spirits. All will be revealed, and you will know what to do for *they* will help you."

"Ok I just need time to take this all in."

"You do not have time; you must be ready now!" Wisdom said to me.

"Ok I got it," I said.

"May we get back to our date?" William asked Wisdom. I could see that he was becoming agitated and that he was ready to leave just as I was. I had heard enough of this nonsense.

"Of course. You have only a few hours left to enjoy before all hell breaks loose."

Chapter 27

William

Here I am standing here kissing the hell out of this beautiful woman when the door opens and this woman with long braids asking us to come into her shop. It's more of a command then anything but she said that she had a message for us.

What in the hell could she reveal to us? I was not scared nor nervous for any soothsayer to tell Kodia that I was in love her. No one on this earth could tell me that it was not love at first sight,

The moment our lips touched I wanted to taste more of her. I wanted to take her far away and just love her. For when our lips met, it felt like I was meant to be the only man to *love* her. I could feel her longing and desire for me, and I knew that there would be no pushing me away from taking her. But then that door opened, and I came back to my senses.

Here I am sitting across from this woman who is telling me, no telling us that we are from a past life and that it is our destiny to be together. That some dark force was trying to destroy her. Just from that revelation all I knew was that I wanted to protect her! And when she grabbed my hands, I could feel another presence around me, and it felt like she was pulling him from me. I could see the love that that man had for that young woman and how he had taken care of her until she died, and it was the same love I had for Kodia.

I did not give a damn about race or anything. She was mines and soon I was going to be hers. I did not have time to listen to anything else. That woman told me that I needed to drink this liquid from that bottle that would turn me into a werewolf and that I would be more powerful.

At first, I was in shock. Who wants to be a werewolf for the rest of their life, but if it was needed to protect the woman that I loved, who gives a fuck! I was ready to do anything for her and to make her realize that I am all that she will ever need.

I heard Kodia cry out to me, but I was not listening to her. But when I looked into her eyes she was crying, and I knew right then and there that she *loved* me. Whether she would ever admit or not, she was connected to me and nothing was going to change that.

Chapter 28

Kodia and William

I was still unable to grasp the thought that Abenaa was out to
destroy me. After our mother had died, she had been all that I had. I
knew that we had family scattered throughout the North Carolina,
but none of then had ever reached out to us. I did not even know
about this woman whom I looked like and that she was a part of my
bloodline. Nothing was making sense to me.

And then William drunk that shit! He could turn into a
werewolf Just to keep me from harm's way. I did not even know
him, but I knew that I loved him. Did I just think that out loud? I
love him! I felt in in my soul and I wanted to be with him. This is all
so crazy and it does not make any sense, but still there must be some
kind of truth to what she was saying because we connected so
quickly.

I glanced over at him and he drove silently in his thoughts.
What was he thinking? Did he really love me like she said he did?

"Beautiful are you okay?" he asked me.

"Yes, I am ok," I answered. "I just have so many thoughts in my head. I am trying not to doubt but to believe."

"I feel you beautiful but everything that she told us is true."

"How do you know? Where is the proof that something bad is waiting to destroy me?"

"I cannot explain it but I just know. When she touched me and took my hands, I felt him. I felt James and I saw no felt the love that he had for *Kente* and I was filled with it."

"William what are you saying?" I asked him, looking at him.

I had no idea where we were, but I saw a sign that read *Scenic Overlook* and I asked him to pull over. He pulled over and parked and I got out of the truck. I walked in front of the truck and I looked up in the sky. I saw so many stars that the mountain tops appeared to be full of light. I felt William walk up and stand beside me.

"This is so beautiful," I said to him softly.

"It is but not as beautiful as you," he replied.

"The poet I see."

"Baby I am not a poet, but I know what I see. You are beyond beauty, but beautiful is the only word I can call you. Kodia I know that you are scared and nervous and trying to grasp the meaning of all this, but I promise you this, if you trust me, I will not let anything happen to you."

I turned and faced him. "William, I have a gift as well. I have never tapped into it. But there have been times in which I felt things. Especially in my dreams. I dreamt that I was with *James* and he was making love to me. But it was not him it was you. So, part of me believes that we are them."

"Kodia we are *them*."

William took me in his arms and began kissing me. I fell into his embrace never wanting him to stop. He picked me up and placed me on the hood of his truck. He began kissing me all over my body and I wanted him to have more. I slid off the truck and walked to the back of the truck. I began taking off my clothes.

"Kodia stop," William said. "I can take you to a room. People will see when they drive by."

"Fuck people!" I exclaimed. "I want you now, anytime anyplace." William lifted me up and carried me to passenger side of the truck. Opening the door with one hand, he laid me down on the seat. His eyes were dark, and I could feel his desire for me. He began kissing me on breasts taking my dark nipples into his mouth and tasting one at a time. I arched my back so that he could taste more, and he began moving down to my waist.

He began kissing on my stomach and then his kisses moved to my thighs. My body was aching for that kiss that would take me over the top. As his lips kissed all around my center, I could feel his beard brushing against my moist lips and then he licked me. It was the must sweetest thing that I had veer felt in my life! His touch was so sweet and tender, and it was if he had never tasted anything as sweet as me before. He spread open my pussy and he began sticking his tongue inside of me. His tongue was flickering on my spot and I could not stop my body from squirting all in mouth. I could feel my juices flowing down his beard and he slurped them up.

"Please William," I whispered to him.

"Please what?" he asked me still tasting me.

"Please make love to me," I answered,

William stood up and slid his pants down. I could see his member standing erect and ready for me. This was the first time that I have ever seen a *white* one before and it was beautiful to me. I opened my legs as he climbed in between them and the moment he slid inside of me; I knew that there was turning back.

Slowly he grinded into me stroking me and bringing me to so many orgasms. He looked down into my face as my juices dripped from his beard and landed on my lips. William licked his lips and then he kissed me. It was so sweet, and I could still feel my walls pulsating and gripping him to keep him inside of me.

"May I come?" he asked me softly.

No man had ever asked me that before. "Yes, my love, " I said to me. "Please come inside of me." He grabbed me tight and pulled me inside of him. I could hear his breathing increasing as he began to pound me harder. I could feel myself about to orgasm as well .

"I love you!" we both exclaimed together as we both came together.

Yes, there was no turning back!

Chapter 29

Abenaa

Mae went back into the house and began cleaning up some of the blood. She did not want Kodia to come back and be alarmed. She wanted her to think that everything was alright. Whether or not *Marinette* had accepted her blood sacrifice or not, she was determined to stop *Kente* from coming thru her blood.

Now William, she did not care if *James* took him over, for she was still in love with *James* and she believed that once he saw her in this young girl's body that he would forget about *Kente* and desire her.

Mae would have to get use this time period that she was in, but that would be so easy to do. It appeared to her that being able to use her powers was a common thing now and done out openly. She would never have to hide from the *white man* again, for they were a free people now and slavery was over. She could create her own religion and have followers and worshipers. All she had to do was absorb their power and be greater than anything they could have ever imagined. Damn she could be greater than *Jesus,* the white man's

god she was forced to believe in. Being able to move freely and do

whatever she wanted to do was what she always wanted for her

people.

People mistook her for being *evil,* but she was not evil. She

just wanted to be able to free her people from slavery and live the

best life that she could live. But other people did not understand her

drive, her zest. She thought that everyone should be like her and

want the *spirits* to empower them so they could be free from

oppression. Okay maybe she did get a little crazy with it, but damn

somebody should.

Mae finished cleaning up as much blood as she could and

change placed a whit sheet over the altar the witches had put

together. Hopefully Kodia would be kind and understand her as

others had not. It would be easy for her to manipulate Kodia because

she did not want the *power* anyway. She glanced around the room

again and was proud of her work. But her energy was draining, and

she decided to go sit in the rocker on the porch and rest.

She glanced up at the sky and the night sky seemed to be lit up by twinkling stars. There was even a full moon and it was so beautiful. "I remember the last full moon that I saw. That night was supposed to be *my* night of glory." Mae spoke out loud to herself. "I really do not know how she was able to steal that drink and give it to *James*. He would have been my protector not hers! I hate that African bitch, and tonight I am going to destroy her beloved Kodia. I am not sparing no one's life. Abenaa I know you can hear me! I am going to destroy you and take over this body right after I kill your sister!" she closed her eyes and began drifting off to sleep. She needed her rest.

As soon as Abenaa felt her drift off she began to try to focus with all her might to call upon *Kente* to help her. Her powers were fading quickly. She tried to take over her to stop her from killing those witches, her friends, but Mae was just to strong. But now that she had drifted off to sleep, she was trying to regain some of her power.

Abenaa was riding a long bus sitting way in the back seat and slowly she began to sit up. If only she could make it to the front of the bus. She knew that if willed herself to get there, she would be able to take control of her body. Each step that she took felt like her feet was sinking in concrete. She remembered the movie she had seen *Get Out* and she would be damn if she was just going to keep drifting into subconsciounesss and staying on that bus.

Abenaa passed the fifth row of seats on the bus and she could feel her strength coming back. "Yes!" she said to herself. "I can do this." As she approached the seventh row of seats, she saw a woman sitting in the ninth seat with a red cloak on covering her face.

"Who are you?" she asked her.

"I do not need for you take over yet," the woman spoke to her.

"I have to fight to save my life and Kodia's," Abenaa said weakly.

"Your life first ha! Still selfish as always," the woman smirked.

Abenaa moved in closer. "Wh-who are you?" she asked

again.

The woman stood up and turned to face Abenaa. Abenaa was taken back by what she saw and fell back against the seat. The woman had long black hair, but her face was skeletal. Her eyes were like fire as well as her hands. It was as if she controlled the element.

"I am the one that most people forget about. But before your time I was *worshipped* by your people. See child, with me comes the fire and freedom. They fear what they do not know, and I have been accused of burning things down. I am just as powerful as my sisters and brothers, but the people only called upon me to be set free from slavery."

The woman walked upon Abenaa and touched her on her face. Abenaa thought the `fire from her hands had burnt her but she was not burned. "*Kente* believed in me and she created my temple. Not like the churches you see today, but out in the woods, out in nature. Some still carry my traditions', but she was the only one to that could hold me. I rode her often."

"If you were my ancestral guide, then you should have been

with me," Abenaa said to her.

"I have always been beside you and your sister. Especially your sister, for she was born to *Kente*'s likeness. But you have always been jealous of her and that is why I only empowered you a little bit."

"Why did you allow Mae to take me?"

"I could not stop that for it was your destiny to teach you a lesson about family. Don't you know child that family is greater together than apart? This was my teaching to *Kente,* and she passed it down. When the time is right I will free Mae from you. But you ain't learnt your lesson yet," the woman said then she disappeared.

"Fuck that shit!" Abenaa said loudly. "I need to be in control!" She tried to stand up and move towards the front of the bus again, but she was immediately flung back to the back of the bus as skeletal hands came out the seat and held her down.

Chapter 30

Kodia

I am walking on a dirt road and I come to a bus. I can see two women on the bus. As I move closer, I see that my sister is sitting down while a woman is standing over. This woman is dressed in slave clothes and she is holding a machete dripped in blood. I move slowly trying to not draw attention to myself because I must save Abenaa from this woman. Just as I approach the bus three women appear covered in blood. I stand still waiting to see what they are going to do. Suddenly I hear Abenaa scream, and I began to run. I do not care if those bloodied women see me or not. When I reach the door of the bus the three women grab me, and I fall back on the ground. They stand over me and I realize that they are the three witches who I had seen in Asheville. They grab me trying to hold me and stop me from getting on the bus. I begin to feel this energy coming in from me the back of my neck and my head begins to hurt. It feels like someone just touched me on the back of my neck. I turn around and the three witches are gone, and I see one woman standing there cloaked in red. Her face is skeletal and fire dances in her eyes. She smiles at me then she moves inside of me and my body feels likes it's on fire

I scream as I jump up from laying beside William. I must have does off after out love making. "Are you okay?" he asks me.

"Yes, I had this crazy dream," I tell him as I reach for my clothes and began to get dressed. "How long was I out for?"

"Five minutes," he said to me.

"Five minutes? Damn you must have knocked me out."

"I slipped on my pants then I just laid back down beside you on the seat. You looked so peaceful," he said to me. "What did you dream?"

"In my dream I saw my sister and there was this old slave woman standing over her with a machete. She must be the *dark force* that has my sister." I told him.

"Why do you say that?"

"They were on this long ass bus, and it looked as if my sister could not move. Also, the three witches that I had seen earlier were in my dream and they were covered in blood. It was as if they were doing her bidding. They were trying to stop me from getting on that bus, but then this skeletal woman appeared with fiery eyes. She touched me on the back of neck and when I turned around, she entered me, and it felt like my body was fire." I reached behind my neck and began rubbing it.

"Turn around beautiful," William said.

I turned around and he lifted my hair. "That was no dream. You have a red mark at the base of your neck."

"Are you sure?" I exclaimed. I jumped in the truck and pulled the rearview mirror down. I reached inside my bag and pulled out my compact mirror. I opened it up and turned my head around so that I could see the back of neck. He was right there was a red mark at the base of neck. It looked like someone had touched me with something hot.

"Now do you believe?" William asked me. "She told you to pay attention to your dreams."

"William, we have to get back to the cottage. My sister is in danger!" I cried.

The tears began streaming down my face and I began praying. I did not care about anything else but making sure that I was there to save my sister.

Chapter 31

Sisters

When we pulled up in front of the cottage everything looked normal. I could see candles flickering from the windows and I smelled smoke. "Do you smell that?" I asked William.

"Yes, it smells like someone was burning food," he answered.

I jumped out of the truck and ran up the stairs and opened the door. William was right behind me and when we both walked in, we saw a white clothed table in the middle of the living room with tall candles burning on it. Abenaa was sitting beside the table and she looked up when she saw us enter the room.

"How was your date?" she asked me, smiling.

"Abenaa are you ok?" I asked her back.

"Yes why?" she said to me.

"We met this woman who told us that you were in trouble," I said.

"Sis you got to stop listening to these fake soothsayers up here. Everyone wants a dollar and they will tell you anything to get you to believe them so you can spend money."

"What is that?" William asked pointing to what looked like blood on the couch.

I walked over to the couch and looked at the stains. "I think that it is blood," I answered. I walked back to William. "Abenaa are you okay, that's blood."

Abenaa stood up and walked over to William. "You really do look just like him." She spoke to him.

"Look like who?" I asked her. Something was off with my sister. And what did she mean by that. She never answered my question.

"*James*," she said.

"So, you do know about our history and about *Kente*?"

Abenaa turned around and looked at me. "Mama told me about *Kente* before she died. She showed me a picture of them. *Kente* and *James*. She told me that you are supposed to inherit all her power."

"What do you mean inherit all her power. You know that you are the one into all that hocus pocus shit, not me."

"Exactly, so it was hard for me to believe that you are the one to get it all."

I heard jealousy in her voice, and I began to realize that Wisdom had been right. My sister was jealous of me, and if that was so, she would destroy me for my gifts.

"Sis, I don't want that shit. I just want to be with William. We had a nice date and I believe we will be good for each other." William moved closer to me and put his arm around me ,pulling me closer to him , he kissed me on my cheek.

At that moment Abenaa's facial expression changed, and I saw nothing there but hate. It was like a dark shadow had fallen all around her and she did not look like my sister. Her face had become dark. "Do you honestly believe that you get to walk out of here with the power and *James*?" she asked me angrily.

"*James*? This is William," I spoke calmly.

"No that's *James*. *Kente* you will not win this time!" she yelled at me.

Suddenly the flames on the candles shot up in the air, and it felt like a burst of hot wind swept thru the room. Dishes began to fall of the shelves and shatter all over the floor. I looked in the mirror hanging on the wall behind Abenaa and I saw a slave woman as her image.

"Who are you?" I asked

"Mae and your *sister* is no longer here!" I watched as she began to levitate off the floor. Raising her hands, she motioned towards a piece of broken glass and it flew my way. William grabbed me and pushed me against the wall. The broken glass barely missed my face. "Are you okay?" he asked me.

"Yes," I answered. I was bit shaken up, but I had no fear.

"Let my sister go!" I yelled at Mae over the turbulence in the room.

Mae floated back to the floor and she placed her hands on her hips. "Let your sister go. Now that will never happen. Do you not realize that your sister wanted me to take her?"

I shook my head in disagreement. "That's not true," I said.

"Oh, chile it is true. She and those witch friends of hers were planning something real special for you tonight. She was going to do a ritual called *switching of the heads* and take your power for her own. That's why it was so easy to posses her. She already had hate in her heart for you, sister."

I could not believe that Abenaa knew all this time who I really was and what was going to happen to me.

"Your dead mama told her what to do, but those witches were going to help her switch it up. Chile, I did you favor by offering those witches up as a blood sacrifice. That's whose blood you saw. Now I got their power."

"Kodia the dream. Remember you told me that they were covered in blood!" William exclaimed.

So, it had been them in the dream. "I want my sister back. Regardless of what you say she is still my blood."

"No, she is mines!" Mae yelled.

William moved towards Mae and with her eyes she flanged him against the wall. He was trying to break free, but he could not free himself. "William," I shouted as I ran towards him.

"*James* isn't that your blood too? You are a foolish man," Mae said with an evil grin on her face.

"My name is not *James!*" William yelled at her. "Let me go!"

"Fuck you!" Mae yelled back. Mae looked at me.

Suddenly, I could feel myself beginning to rise and I realized that Mae was controlling my body with her mind. I was ascending off the floor and I had no usage of my limbs. I floated over to the table and fell hitting the table with a thud. Dark dirty hands began coming from the table and they were holding me down. All I could think of was my dream, and how I was trying to escape them. I could hear William cries telling her to let me go. I glanced over at Mae and she was coming at me with a machete. I tried to speak but no sound escaped my mouth. Mae took the top of the machete and she cut me on my wrist. I could see the blood oozing from my veins . I closed my eyes and when I opened them *Kente* was standing over me. "Let me in," she whispered to me.

I nodded my head and then I felt this feeling like fire enter my body. Now I was on the bus.

Chapter 32

The Bus

I was on the same bus that had been in my dreams. But there was no Abenaa just me and I was sitting in the back seat, while *she* Kente, was the driver. I felt strange but she felt familiar. It was as if part of my being had taken a seat while the other half had taken control. Its hard to explain, but I had no fear. It was like I *was* her.

I tried to stand up and move closer to her, but I could not move. This did not scare me for I knew that Kente would not hurt me. I began to understand that Abenaa had been taken over by Mae when I saw them on *her* bus. I was attempting to save her, but then I had gotten stop. If I had gotten home a lot sooner, I would have been able to help her fight.

"No. you could not have stopped Mae from taking her," I heard a woman's voice say to me. Standing in front of me was the skeleton woman I had also seen in my dreams.

"Who are you?" I asked her.

"Marinette," she replied.

"Why did you prevent me from helping my sister!" I exclaimed.

"You had not yet merged with Kente. Your sister Abenaa needed to be taught a lesson. Everything my disciple told you was the truth. She is very jealous of and you and she wanted the power."

"I do not want this. She is the one who has always been in tune with this spiritual shit," I said. "I just wanted to be happy and live my life knowing that my sister would always be my by side."

"You will live your life and she will be by your side. Kente has always been a part of you. She came back to destroy Mae from ending her bloodline. I am the one who will give you your power just like I did Kente. Your ancient ancestors believed in us and I have always been with your bloodline. I work with people who want to work with me and understand my power. Mae offered those witches as a burnt offering to me, but it was not accepted. Look into my eyes."

I looked into *Marinette's* eyes and her flames jumped into me. I felt like I could control the flames and I needed to regain control of myself. I stood up and I began to move towards to the

front of the bus. As soon as I got to the driver's seat, Kente looked at

me and she saw the flames dancing in my eyes. She got up and I

took the wheel.

Chapter 33

Fight a spirit with a spirit

I came to and I could see the blood still flowing my arms. I began to focus with my mind and the cut began to heal itself. I jumped off the table with my newfound strength and pushed Mae against the wall.

"My, my, my," Mae said smirking. "I see that *Kente* has empowered you."

"No, it was *Marinette,*" I said through my teeth.

"That can not be. I gave her a burnt offering and *she* was supposed to help me," she said.

"Bitch your offerings are not accepted by her. You will let my sister go, and you will go back to hell from where you came from!" I yelled.

"Who do you think you are commanding, me?" Mae said to me. Closing her eyes, she began chanting in a language that I had never heard of and the floor began to split in two. I jumped to avoid falling thru the crack and then I saw William. He had been freed from what was holding him and he was able to jump across the split to stand by my side. Mae clapped her hands and the roof of the cabin blew off almost hitting William's truck. We could see the night sky and the full moon.

"Something is happening to me," William said, his voice shaking.

I watched as William flung his head back in pain and fell to the floor. I could see him writhing around on the floor. I knelt beside him. "William," I said placing my hands on his shoulder.

"Don't touch me!" he cried out in pain.

I moved away from him as he began to scream out in pain, as his body convulsed and it felt like I could feel all his pain as his flesh began to rip apart.

Mae had jumped over the split and she held the machete high in the air. Just as she swung the machete down towards my head, a huge wolf lunged at her and pinned her down to the floor. William had become he wolf! Mae began fighting the beast trying to free herself from his clutches. The wolf began ripping chunks out of her arm with his claws.

"No!" I screamed for that was my sister's body. The wolf stopped and looked at me. "That is still my sister."

Slowly the wolf began backing away from Mae as she regained herself and stood up. She waved over her arm and the wounds had vanished.

"*Marinette* if you are with me, help me!" I said. I began to feel the fire inside of me and when I looked at Mae, fire came from my eyes and made a circle around her. I walked to her and stepped through the flames. Grabbing the back of Abenaa's head, I placed my hands on the back of her neck and snatched Mae from her body. Abenaa fell to the floor.

Suddenly my mouth opened, and a huge flame sprouted forth like a whirlwind. I saw *Kente* step out the flame. "It takes a spirit to fight a spirit," she said to me.

Mae tried to flee through the top of the cottage but Kente had grabbed her.

"You have always wanted to destroy me, now that same

destruction that you had for me will be your downfall," *Kente* said to her.

"Let me go!" Mae cried.

Kente opened her mouth and swallowed Mae's soul.

Chapter 34

Us

I rushed over to Abenaa trying to wake her up. I prayed that she had not died and that her soul had not been with Mae. Slowly she began to come to, and helping her to her feet I walked her to the couch to sit down. As I was helping her, the wolf had turned back into William and he was placing what was left of his clothes back on. *Kente* had moved towards Abenaa and I and she hugged us.

"Thank you for helping us *mama*," I said to her as tears streamed down my face. I could not stop the water from flowing my eyes. It seemed liked all my emotions hit me at once and I could not stop crying.

"Is she coming back?" Abenaa asked. Her voice was very weak ashe was trying to regain her strength.

"No, she will not be back," *Kente* said to her. "Mae is in a place where she needs to be. Maybe one day she will come back , but as far as trying to repossess you and take you over, no."

I could still feel *Marinette* inside of me and she spoke to my sister. *"Now have you learned your lesson?"*

"Yes," Abenaa answered. "I need to respect all that is and be accepting of my own gifts."

"Yes daughter," *Kente* replied. "For by your actions you caused the death of three of my disciples and they loved me so much that their lives ended. The power that you are seeking and wanted from your sister is yours to share. You are both part of me and it will continue to flow through all my daughters."

"But why did *mom* not tell me about you and who *I* was? Why did she only tell Abenaa?"

Kente looked at me. "Abenaa has always believed in the ancestors and the spirit world. You believed a little bit, and your mother was afraid that you would reject your heritage. Abenaa was supposed to wake you up to your power, not try to take it."

"I'm so sorry for all that has happened," Abenaa said weeping.

"It's ok," I said to her, comforting her.

"No, it's not okay. I have been so jealous of you, and that

jealousy cause me to be an easy target for Mae. I could have killed

you! *She* could have killed you!" she cried.

"But you didn't. *She* didn't. I truly understand it all. The

dreams that I had been having were the ancestors waking me and

telling what I needed to pay attention to. I love you Abenaa."

William walked over to me and placed his arm around my

shoulder. *Kente* turned to face us.

"You and he do look like us, but you are not us. We did not

reincarnate inside of you, but we walk with you," *Kente* said to us.

"Will I always be a werewolf?" William asked *Kente*.

"Yes, you will be. But you will be able to control the change.

Your job is to protect them because not only are they my daughters,

but they are daughters of *Marinette* as well. The werewolves protect

her and her children. You will be able to live a normal life. *James*

did with me and look at what our children produced."

I glanced up at William and he was smiling.

"Kodia you have been chosen to take care of the spirits in our

family. That right has been given to you. It will be up to you to make sure that we are remembered, and that the bloodline keeps the tradition. Abenaa you will help her, but you will be the healer. You already do readings and you help others," *Kente* said to us.

"Trust in your abilities and know that we are here to guide you. Because you look like me you will find people who will want to follow you like they did me. This came from trusting in my ancestors and *Marinette*. You will always be able to speak to me and even your mother. Do not believe in anything man made but follow your intuition and create. The power is yours to be able to create anything that you want as long as it is not being done for selfish reasons."

Abenaa cast her head down.

"Abenaa do not do that. You have learnt and from this experience you will be able to help others you wanted to travel a darker path, and there is nothing wrong with that. You must learn how to balance out both sides of who you are. Working with the spirits and gaining power is not about being rich and famous. It has to be a way of life."

"I understand, *mama*," Abenaa said.

Kente closed her eyes and began chanting in her native tongue. Suddenly, the cottage was made back whole, and it looked the cottage had never been touched. "I love you both and I have to leave. Make sure you give offerings constantly and set something up for *Marinette*. Allow her to talk to you about what she wants, and you will go far."

I nodded my head in agreement then Kente was gone. I could not feel the fire inside of me, but I knew that when the time comes, I will feel it again.

Chapter 35

Kodia

As I stared out the window at the Smoky Mountains, I began

to smile. This weekend was a weekend to remember. I had been

awakened to my ancestors , to the spiritual world and the truth.

Everything that I thought could not exist, existed and the fear that I

once felt has disappeared. Not to say that there will not be times

when I will be nervous, but if I have the love of my people backing

me whom shall, I fear?

I glanced over at William as he kept fiddling with the radio

trying to find some music he wanted to listen to. He took my hand in

his and kissed it. I could get use to riding with him and seeing parts

of the United States that I had never seen. We were on our way to

Knoxville, and I told Abenaa that I was going with him.

At first, she was upset because of all that we had experienced

and did not want to be alone., but I told her that I would be back

during the middle of the week. I explained to her that I wanted to get

to know him more and add on to the love that I was feeling for him. I no longer cared that he was not of my race! I loved him and I did not want to leave his side.

I took my cell phone from my bag and went to Amazon shopping. I wanted to buy a new journal to record all the visions that would be coming to me now that I had awaken what was dormant in my DNA. I also wanted to record all my journeys with William.

As I stared at him, his countenance had changed. His beard seemed to have grown longer and there was a white strip running down the center of it. His hair looked a little bushier, and he was really looking sexier to me. It appeared like he had more strength, more confidence in himself. Maybe it had something to do with his shape shifting into a werewolf. All I knew was that he would never allow anyone or anything to hurt me.

I moved closer to him, as I did, I could feel heat coming from him. "Baby you feel so warm," I said to him.

William gave me a mischievous smile. "You moved closer to me and it got me all warm," he said. "Keep it up and the beast is going to come out." He growled at me.

I started laughing. "You do not want this fire!"

I looked up into the rearview mirror as fire danced in my eyes.

Author's Note

I would like to take this time to thank everyone who took the time to read my book. I love the mountains and I have always felt so spiritual when I visited them. As I was writing this book and researching the area, I found out that there really were white slave masters who married their African slaves and move to the mountains. There they lived amongst the Native Americans and mingled. I did not know this before I wrote this book. If in any way parts of my book reflects on the history of a family during that era, I meant no harm.

This book is fictional, and the characters are all fictional. The narrative of this book was given to me in a dream. If the Ancestors are wanting me to tell part of a tale of someone's life so that their story may be heard, I truly give thanks!

Queen

Special Acknowledgements:

I would like to thank Kenaz Filan and Raven Kaldera for their book titled **Drawing Down the Spirits: The Traditions and Techniques of Spirit Possession.** By reading your book I was able to have a better understanding of my own spiritual possessions.

Chapter 7

Spirit and Flesh

How Possession Works

It is one of the best ways to experience divinity, It shoves your face in the fact that there is something bigger than you, right in front of you, every day. It is a far wilder and more personal experience of divinity that other methods I have experienced.

- **Summerwind Tashlin, Pagan spirit-worker**

This whole chapter helped me tremendously. Thank you!!!

Made in the USA
Middletown, DE
05 November 2023

41908517R00116